AF432955

Quantum Quirks: A Science Fiction Childhood

The Cassidy Chronicles

Adam Gaffen

Published by Adam Gaffen, Author, LLC, 2024.

Also by Adam Gaffen

Godsfall
The Book of One
The Book of Two
The Book of Three
A Roman Holiday
Godsfall: Books 1-3
Sherlock Holmes and the Case of the Lazarus Conspiracy

Tales from the Cassidyverse
Into the Black
The Heart of Space
The Shape of the Fire
Midnight Relics

The Artemis War
The Road to the Stars
The Measure of Humanity
A Quiet Revolution

Triumph's Ashes

The Cassidy Chronicles
Run Like Hell
The Cassidy Chronicles - The Spark Before the Fire
Terran Federation Technical Manual
The Eternity Protocol: Complete Duology
Shades of Rose: Becoming
Shades of Rose: Breaking
The Girl in the Scope
Quantum Quirks: A Science Fiction Childhood
Embers of Eternity
Shades of Rose: Complete Duology

The Covenant
Shadow Bound

The Missions of the TFS Pike
The Ghosts of Tantor
Tracking Tantor

Standalone
The Kildaran
Roots of Love

Refuge
The Artemis Wars Omnibus
The Vault & The Vixen
Death Gets an Upgrade
Whispers in the Fog: Two Unpublished Holmes Mysteries
Dating to Die For
The Catacombs That Creep and Crawl

Watch for more at www.adamgaffenauthor.com.

Table of Contents

Author's Note

HEY THERE.

This is a collection of my memories of Aiyana from our childhood, going back as early as I can recall and ending, well, no spoilers. If you want, you can call it a sideways autobiography, or a memoir, or something. I've never been bothered by labels, so I don't know why I'd start now.

Are there gonna be gaps? Of course! You have to remember that I'm trying to recall all this across a couple centuries worth of memories; if I can't dredge it up it myself, I'm not going to outside sources. I want you to have *my* memories, not someone else's. Well, with the exception of Cass. If she was there, and she was for most of this, then I'll let her supplement what I know.

I'm going to try to keep this in more-or-less chronological order, with a few caveats. If one story leads me naturally to another, I'm going to tell it. And if there's a bit in there which jumps tracks and references something in the future, I'm also going to leave it.

Look, this is really informal writing. It's not what I do for a living and not something I have much experience with. I don't want to have it polished up and turned into some kind of pompous history of the Federation's founder! That's not who I was when I did this, and it's not something I set out to do. It just sort of happened along the way.

I think that's enough caveats. I really just want to tell you my stories, because I think it shows how far back Cass and I were special to each other.

Get ready. You won't be bored. How much trouble could two independent, curious, intelligent girls have gotten into in 2080s Minnesota, after all?

As it turns out...

From my mind to yours, my memories of Aiyana.

Kendra Cassidy

Admiral, Terran Federation (Ret.)

Introduction

IT HAS OCCURRED TO me, somewhat belatedly perhaps, that while I have spent months, years even, with Adam, telling him stories about the people who I've become close to in my *mumble-mumble* years leading the Federation, I haven't mentioned Aiyana. At least, not our private lives, not our lives before Farrell took a shot at her at our wedding. I mean, she is my wife, after all; I've known her all my life, or at least near enough, so I have all these great stories to tell but haven't shared any of them!

She was born three weeks before me, a fact that she has never let me forget. Frankly, I don't think that's fair; after all, it's not like either of us had any control over our birthdays, but you try reasoning with her on it! Whenever she and I disagree about something, and she can't convince me through logic, she pulls out the "I'm older than you" card as a last resort.

Not. Fair.

It's also not fair that she ended up almost ten centimeters taller than me, has the most beautiful, silky, long, auburn hair, or pale, ice-blue eyes that still pull me in to their crystalline depths.

Totally not fair.

Of course, she also had to deal with her parents, and they were challenging. Maybe it's fairer to say that their circumstances were challenging.

Okay, I'm going to have to explain this.

We all lived in the Northern Imperium. That was good, in some ways, but bad in a bunch of ways. The Daley Family ruled, rules, will rule, the Imperium pretty strictly. They don't take well to challenges to their authority, in any form, and that includes protests. Well, when her parents were younger, they were involved in the student protests back in the 60s and early 70s. Nothing happened to them, overtly, but their names were taken by the Imperial Internal Affairs Bureau.

As they planned for their wedding, they applied for visas for their honeymoon and were denied permission to leave. That was the first they knew of the problems they had, but it wasn't the last.

Anyways, this isn't about them; it's about Aiyana and me and the adventures we had.

You know, I don't know anyone who calls her Aiyana. It's a beautiful name, and one of my favorite things about her, but even I don't call her Aiyana, or not often. I think I might use her proper name once in any given week, usually to get her attention, and that includes when I proposed to her and our wedding.

She was born brilliant. I am utterly convinced of that. That was a blessing and a curse. Cass was so bored in our classes at school! At least for the first couple years, we shared classes, and she just absorbed all the information the teachers were trying to pour into us. That is, when she wasn't telling them they were wrong! And I hated it, because later she would go off to the advanced classes in the afternoon and do stuff and leave me behind.

There was an upside. It made me work harder, because on the way home she was always so happy and bubbly and excited about what she had learned that day, and none of it made sense to me because she was doing things I wouldn't get to for years but it didn't matter.

So here we go. Let's see if I can keep my stories straight!

Prelude - Aiyana's Valentine

I REMEMBER MY FIRST Valentine's Day in school.

There were seventeen of us, all five or six years old, and in the days leading to The Day the teacher made sure we all made enough little cards so every person in the class would get one. He showed us what to write, too. I think it was "Friends are special people," or something similarly insipid, at any rate.

Anyhow, there were two people in my class who I wanted to give special notes to, Aiyana and Allen. I know, I know. Two people, and this is supposed to be about Cass and me, so I hear you saying, who's Allen?

He was a friend of mine for years and years and years; he and I never quite had a romance, but he was certainly the big brother I never had. I've told the story of what happened to him as an adult elsewhere; I'll let you find it on your own.

After I finished the cards the teacher wanted me to make I started doing two more.

I wish I had a picture of them. I don't know what happened to Allen's; Aiyana tells me that she kept hers, but it's probably at her parents' home in the Imperium. Anyways, I covered them with flowers and hearts and rainbows. I know, very cliche, but I was five! I hid them in my desk, and on The Day - it was a Thursday - I added them to the pile, down at the bottom so I wouldn't mix them up.

I went around the room, just like all the other kids, putting a card on every desk, and when I got to my two special Valentines I made sure their cards wouldn't be missed. Once I finished and went back to my desk, I find a pile or cards for me, just like everyone else's. Maybe it was unkind, but I flipped through them all, looking for ones from Allen or Aiyana.

Allen's was easy to find; he wrote, 'GOOBER!' in big letters.

Aiyana's, though - I look and look and look, and there's her school-approved one, and it says what all the others say.

I tell you, my heart breaks.

Then, as I'm sitting there, miserable, she walks up behind me and wraps me in a hug. I like it, but I'm still not happy. I mean, I made her this special card, right? And I get back the one everyone gets?

I don't say anything, though, not then. At recess, we're out in the playground, and she comes up to me. She says, "Why are you mad at me, Kendra?"

Well, I couldn't deny it, so I blurted it out, all of it, in a rush which I don't think anyone except another five-year-old could have understood.

She did, and she laughed. Now I'm mad! She's laughing at me?

Before I can stomp off, she grabs me - she was taller, even then - and wraps me up, and says, 'But Kendra, you know I love you. You're my bestest friend, and that's forever and ever."

"You didn't give me a special card!" I sniffle. "I gave you one!"

"And I love it."

"Why didn't you make one for me?"

And this is when I knew, *knew*, that I loved her. (Yes, I know, five years old. Sue me. I know what I know.)

She says, laughing again - and she has just the best laugh, I don't care what you say, it's like a symphony and joy and birds and sunshine all wrapped into one - "Because I love you, silly, and I don't love them, but I like them and don't want their feelings to be hurt."

That was the end of my bad mood.

Aiyana's Birthday

MAYBE I SHOULD START from the beginning if I'm going to tell Aiyana's story instead of jumping around. Oops.

Aiyana Rosewind Cassidy was born on the 23rd of September, 2080, in East Grand Forks, in the Northern Imperium. Her folks lived in a tiny speck called Key West, a cruel joke if you've ever been to the one in the New Confederacy. I have, and coming home was a nightmare!

Actually, I ought to tell you a funny story which nobody ever seems to know. During the Nameless War (2078), Key West declared its independence from the New Confederacy. They'd long called themselves the Conch Republic, and they took advantage of the Confederacy's distraction to put it into action. They used the leverage they retained by having a United States naval base still on the island to push it through the final settlement. Thus, as a tiny codicil of the treaty which ended the war, Key West became an independent nation. They're usually overlooked in any sociopolitical discussions and they're perfectly happy to keep it that way.

Okay, so maybe I'm the only one who finds it funny. You can look it up, if you want!

Right. Key West, Northern Imperium. That's where we were.

That's where Aiyana grew up, with her parents and an older brother, Shawn. I was born three weeks later, a fact she never lets me forget. She was even more of a brat back then because she got to have her birthday first, something which annoyed me no end. I think I asked my parents every year for four or five years if we could move my birthday earlier, and they always told me that it was when it was and we couldn't change that.

Our parents were neighbors, and so we fell together naturally almost from the start. My dad has way too many holos of the two of us toddling around together, holding hands.

Her folks were hamstrung by their college protests and the attention they received from the IAB. Because of those youthful indiscretions, neither were able to get positions which matched their education or abilities. Both ended up as teachers in the back end of the Imperium. Lesson learned, they stepped back from their previous activism and concentrated on raising their children.

Cass was reading by the time she was three, doing simple math soon thereafter, and started on multiplication and division before she turned four. By her fifth birthday she was using the network to learn algebra and geometry, and her parents were scared.

I was thrilled. All I knew was my best friend was smart and funny and nice to be around. She always made me laugh, and that was enough for me.

My parents, well, they were nice, but they were older. Hal Briggs, my dad, was retired from the Imperium Air Force; Jane Foster, my mom and always Mama to me, was an astrophysicist and geek. She's where I got my love of all things 20th and 21st century, by the way.

They took me in, fostered me, when they were already in their sixties, a few days after I was born. I was essentially an only child, even though I had siblings who ranged in age from twenty-three to thirty-eight (at the time). Hell, my siblings were the same ages as Aiyana's parents, fer gossake, so it's no wonder I felt more at home with her and hers.

We were nearly inseparable.

Our abilities meshed so well, we didn't compete in anything. She was smart, I was a fast thinker. She was tall, but I could jump higher. She remembered stories, but I could tell better jokes, though how good a joke any three- and four-year-old tells is debatable.

Ham and eggs. Peanut butter and jelly. We just fit, right from the start.

One of my first memories that's not a fragment is from her fourth birthday, and her brother had just done something really mean to her. How do I know it was mean? She came running to me, wailing and blubbering, and practically threw herself into me. I just about managed to catch her – I think I mentioned she was always taller than me, which I never thought fair, being taller and older – and turned the almost-fall into sitting down.

"What's wrong?" I asked as she clung to me.

"Shawn!" is all I could understand, but she was shaking and crying and that's enough for me.

Impulsive me, I put her down and go find her brother; Shawn's two years older than us and about six centimeters taller. He's in the kitchen, laughing, I assume about what he just did to his sister, and I totally lose what little control I had. Did I care that there were adults milling around? No, not at all. I picked him up and tossed him across the kitchen, slamming into the outside door, then jumped on him and got in his face. I started yelling, "What did you do to Cass?"

He didn't answer, because I'm also trying to slap him and he's covered up. My dad twigged that something's wrong, lifted me off, and took me home. That was the end of the birthday party for me. I spent the rest of the day, and night, crying.

Early the next day, I woke up with someone holding me. It was Aiyana; she'd snuck over, figured out how to get into the house, and came up the stairs to climb into my bed.

I must've gone back to sleep; the next I knew my mom was yelling about Aiyana being there and telling dad to call her parents and tell them not to worry.

The. Best. Memory. Well, one of them.

School Days 1

BACK TO MY FAVORITE subject. Well, one of my favorite subjects.

I can't imagine what school would have been like without Aiyana. I've said to everyone who would listen how we've always seemed to mesh; we've always been the best parts of each other, even when we were too little to know about any of those sorts of things.

School wasn't any different.

Cass wasn't shy, but she always let the other kids approach her first.

Now that I look back, I wonder if that wasn't because of the bond we shared? I mean, we had each other, we lived next door, we did almost everything together; what need did she have for other kids? I don't think there were any kids from our neighborhood, such as it was. Remember, this was Nowhere, Northern Imperium, and there were more chickens than people in our village.

Me, I was always the first one going around and talking to anyone, no matter how quickly they tried to run away. I was always faster on my feet, which meant I was always the first person picked in games where speed was an asset.

Um.

Sorry, I know, my mind tends to wander when I'm doing these things. That's what happens when you're looking back a couple centuries.

Right. I was talking about the other kids. I always made sure I dragged Aiyana along with me to talk to them. Like I said, she wasn't shy, but she was patient, and she would wait forever for someone to approach her. Me, I was never patient, so I short-circuited all of that.

One girl decided she didn't like me, but she'd hang out with Aiyana any day. That was fine; I wasn't jealous or anything. Looking back, the lengths she'd go to avoid me were funny. It would go something like this: she walked up to Aiyana, started chatting, and then would ask to go play somewhere else. She'd pull Aiyana along, and they'd be happily playing but she'd be looking my way to make sure I wasn't following. If I even looked like I was walking over there, she'd grab Aiyana and drag her somewhere else.

I wonder if she had a crush on Aiyana?

It didn't matter; Aiyana was always there, no matter what. I was all of five, and certainly wasn't looking for love, but I knew what love was because it was shown to me every day.

Even then she was a bloody genius. I've already told you about her reading, and her math. It definitely set her apart, though, and it wasn't just the kids who noticed. Our teacher, Miss Rasczak, felt threatened, if you can believe it. She looked at what Cass did, seemingly without effort, and was convinced Aiyana was cheating, somehow. Of course she couldn't figure out how, because Cass wasn't, but there you go.

It all came to a head about a month into the year. We were sitting, listening to the teacher read a book, and Aiyana told her she'd mispronounced a word. I don't know if Miss Rasczak was having a bad day, but she said she'd had enough and was going to get to the bottom of it. She pulled Aiyana up and marched her down to the office; I followed, because Cass was my best friend and nobody told me not to.

"This girl is trouble!" she said, dumping Aiyana into a chair.

"What did she do?"

"She was rude and disrespectful to me in front of the class!"

Aiyana wasn't saying anything; she was sobbing.

"What did she do?" repeated the principal.

I could see the teacher didn't want to say anything, so I spoke up. "She said that Miss Rasczak said a word wrong!"

"Miss Smith –" I was still a foster child at the time, and hadn't been officially adopted yet. In retrospect, it could have been worse. They could have called me "Kendra Doe."

"Miss Smith, why are you here?"

"Because Miss Rasczak is being mean to my best friend!" I'm sure I wasn't quite as dignified as I want to remember I was.

"I see." He looked from her to me and to Aiyana, still crying. "What did Aiyana do?"

"Miss Rasczak was reading, and Aiyana raised her hand, and then Miss Rasczak called on her and Aiyana said that she said a word wrong and it was pronounced different. Then Miss Rasczak pulled her from her seat and came here."

"I see," he repeated in a sterner voice. "Miss Rasczak, is that accurate?"

"That Cassidy child has been cheating all year long! There's no way she knows the things she knows!"

"That's not the point right now, Miss Rasczak. Is what Miss Smith said accurate? Miss Cassidy raised her hand and corrected your pronunciation?"

She colored. "Well, more or less."

He stood up and came around to kneel in front of Aiyana. "Miss Cassidy. You're not in trouble."

Aiyana looked up, eyes wet. "I'm not?"

"No. Tell me what you said to Miss Rasczak."

"We were sitting in reading time, and she said expresso because it's in the book, but it's not said that way, so I put up my hand and I told her it's espresso, and then...then..."

"It's okay, Miss Cassidy. You did just fine. Miss Smith," he said, looking at me. "Will you take her back to class?"

I nodded. The principal and I were old friends already; I never was much for following rules.

"Miss Rasczak, could I have a word with you?"

The rest of that day was really quiet; the next week, they started doing all kinds of tests to see just where Aiyana was in her learning. We got lucky. Miss Rasczak didn't hold a grudge; she was just stressed and made a bad choice. She learned from it and taught there for years.

But she never questioned Cass's abilities the rest of the year.

The Barn

I'M GOING TO BORE YOU some more, I think.

How interesting can it possibly be to read about two little girls growing up in the back end of nowhere? I mean, we loved it, but we had each other and our families and all the things that can fascinate a kid.

For example, Aiyana's parents grew all their own vegetables. They had a greenhouse, which was actually bigger than their home, and so she grew up with fresh anything all the time. Since I was her best friend and lived next door, I got all the same stuff. Boy, was that a shock when I moved away and had to go shopping for myself! I mean, strawberries in December ought to be tender and sweet and juicy and a beautiful ruby red, right? That's what I was used to. Yeah, those things in the market aren't strawberries, I don't care what they call them.

They grew fresh fruit and vegetables all year, and we always went in and helped ourselves to whatever they had marked off for us. They were good about that, out of necessity. They didn't want us randomly grabbing whatever, but they also wanted her to have good, fresh food, so they set aside an area for us and grew food which was easy for us to grab and munch. Anything there, we could have.

If it was a century earlier, they would have been called hippies. The idea of being self-sufficient and as independent from the government as possible strongly appealed to them. After all, they knew too well what happened when government intruded on citizens' private lives. As a result, they were on the grid, but had a solar farm which was big enough to power the entire place and then some. When I was about four, they added more capacity to their farm and hooked my folks' home into their grid, so we never had a cold, dark, powerless winter night again. That was nice; it was fun snuggling with my cat under the covers as long as she'd stay, but not so much fun seeing my breath in my bedroom.

They also had chickens running around, eating all the scraps the family produced, plus bugs and frogs and anything else their tiny tyrannosaurus beaks could catch. During the winter they stayed in a barn with the rest of the livestock, who lived their best possible lives. They collected eggs, and milked the cows, sheared and got what milk they could from the sheep. Have you ever tried to milk a sheep who didn't want you to? They're mean!

It was a fun place to visit and hang out, and we girls had the run of it.

One day, and it must have been early spring because there was still snow on the ground, we were playing in the barn. There was a lingering smell of animals, cut by the cool spring air and overlaid by hay, and we were running around in the loft. I think we were playing tag.

She said, "I'm thirsty. I'm getting a drink." We had drinks down below.

"Aww, I was about to tag you!"

"I'll be right back, and I'll be it, okay?"

I lit up at that. I could keep away from her just about forever; she was taller, even then, but I was faster.

She was heading for the ladder, and I turned to tell her that was fine so I saw what happened. She wasn't looking where she was going and she put her foot down right on a patch of old hay, dusty and slippery. Her leg went out from under her. Naturally, she fell, but she her tumble sent her flying past the hatch, towards the edge of the loft and over!

"Kendra!" she screamed as she fell.

She managed to catch the edge of the floor with one hand. Her other hand grabbed at the wood but kept snatching hay.

"Kendra!" she yelled again.

I broke out of my freeze and sprinted, then dove flat-out for her hand, sliding on the same hay. Yeah, I know, dumb, but I was five. I just knew Aiyana was in danger and I had to get to her, fast, and jumping seemed faster.

I reached for her hand with mine, grabbing it as her fingers let go and clasped around my wrist, then dug my other hand's fingernails into the wood of the floor so I didn't go over too. We hung there for about half of eternity, one hand clinging to hers, one hand splintering wood.

"I've got you," I panted.

"I knew you would." There was a world of confidence in her voice. "Pull me up?"

"In a minute." Rescuing damsels in distress was something new for me and I hadn't worked out all the details.

"As long as you got me, but maybe hurry?"

I tested my grip and gave a tentative tug upward. No good. I tried again, with more effort, and brought her a few centimeters before I had to relax. Defeated, I said, "I don't think I can. I'm not strong enough."

"Kendra, let your arm come down," she said. She'd been thinking too, you see.

"Huh?"

"I need you to swing your arm."

This didn't sound right to me at all. "Swing my arm? You'll fall!"

"No, I won't. You'll see."

I inched along the boards until the arm holding her was all the way over, the wood digging into my armpit. Both of her hands clutched my wrist, and my hand wrapped around her right wrist. My body was parallel to the edge, and that was as close as I wanted to get.

"I'm going to start swinging now," she said, very calm. "You help me with your arm."

I got what she was describing, so we started her swinging, and each time she got a little bit higher. Back and forth, back and forth, over and over. I thought my arm was going to give out, and I was going to tell her we had to try something else. Before I could, she said, "Next one, biggest swing you can do, all the way around!"

I trusted her, and she had a plan, so I did the biggest swing I could. Up and over the edge she came, letting go of my wrist at the top of the arc and going sailing away from the edge to land in a thump.

"You okay?" I asked, scrambling over and away from the drop.

She was giggling.

"That was fun!"

"Fun? You could have fallen! You'd be in big trouble with your dad!"

Yes, that's what was on my mind. Broken bones? Internal injuries? Nothing, compared to the Wrath of Dad.

"No," she said. "I knew you wouldn't let me fall."

We learned from our close call. The rest of the game was played on the lower level, that day, and we decided none of our parents needed to know.

The Bikes

THAT WAS THE SPRING we got bikes.

Isn't that a sort of rite of passage? Being five or six years old and getting your first bike?

If it is, then we may have made a mistake with our kids, decades later. By the time our oldest was five, we were living full-time on *Njord* and *Enterprise*. No room for bikes, especially on the starship. On the other hand, they learned how to do all sorts of things in low gravity we never had a chance to, so I guess it all worked out.

Yeah, so there we were. It was a couple months after the barn incident, and if you know anything about Minnesota weather you know that May is when things finally turn and winter relaxes its grip on the land. Most of the snow has melted, the occasional reinforcement doesn't last long, and the mud is giving way to growing things. The fields suddenly turn green instead of brown, and seemingly overnight all the trees are covered with leaves. The downside is it rains three days out of four, which meant it was no fun for a couple girls who'd rather be out than in.

But it was spring, and we were five, and so our parents decided it was time for bikes.

They were nice bikes. Mine was green, and Aiyana's was blue. She pouted because she wanted a red one to match her hair, but then her dad pointed out that the blue matched her eyes and she was all smiles again. I'd already noticed and grinned.

"Your bike's the same color as your eyes, Kendra!" she told me. She noticed, too.

For the first week, we went out every day after school, rain, snow, or shine. Part was the newness, and part was the implicit promise of freedom. Our folks allowed us to go anywhere. For five-year-olds, they had trust we wouldn't do anything too stupid. Cass was the responsible one, but I generally didn't get into too much trouble when we were together. She was a good example, and pretty persuasive, talking me out of a bunch of dumb ideas over the years. Another reason we could go out at will was where we lived: nowhere! There simply wasn't much opportunity for anything bad to happen to us, at least not from another person.

We had to watch out for cows.

Spring went on, and we got closer and closer to the end of school. The days got longer, meaning we could stay out later. It was glorious. We were out in all weather, and we'd come home wet and muddy and tired and cranky because we didn't want to take a bath. Mama always insisted I did, probably because there was enough dirt on me to lay down a new field.

Once Saturday morning I went over like I always did, right after breakfast, and found Aiyana arguing with her mom. It was really pouring down, and going to get worse, so her mom forbade us from going out. I didn't mind; I was never that much a fan of the weather. Aiyana, though, she was really frustrated.

That's when Cass got her bright idea, and she dragged me along.

She asked her dad, all innocence, if she could tinker with our bikes to make them better. I don't know what he thought she meant, but he agreed. Then she asked if she could use some of the stuff they had stored in the barn, and he agreed to that too. There were always had a bunch of leftover equipment and parts in the barn, what with one thing and another. Then – and he really should have known better at this point – she asked if she could use his tools. I don't know what he thought she meant. Hammer? Screwdriver? Wrench? Well, he agreed, and that was it.

First she studied those bikes for about ten minutes. I swear she was memorizing where every bolt and screw went, how it all fitted together, and how it was all supposed to work. Once she was done, she went into the house and came back with a pile of scrap paper and a pencil, which she handed to me. Then she started taking them apart.

She'd undo a bolt or a screw or something, hand it to me, and tell me what to write down. I'd scribble and hand it to her, and she'd put it under the piece. And again. And again. In about thirty minutes we had two bikes, carefully labeled, scattered across half the barn floor.

"Cass?" I probably sounded worried. This was my bike, my first taste of freedom, and it looked like it was never going anywhere again.

"Don't worry, Kendra. I know what I'm doing."

That was good enough for me.

We went hunting through the junk for parts. I didn't know what we were really looking for; she'd describe what she wanted, and I'd do my best to find it. Pretty soon we had another pile of parts we'd found, and she got to work.

A few minutes of running back and forth between the parts and her dad's toolbox frustrated her. Cass tried to pull it over, but it was a foot taller than she was and weighed more than both of us put together, so she needed my help. Between us we managed it, and she started pulling out all sorts of tools. There were the ones he thought she'd use, but there were power tools too. I recognized a drill, and a laser joiner, some sort of grinder thingy, and others which I still don't have names for.

That's when she really dove in. Over the next four hours, with a break for lunch and my eager but untrained assistance, she put the bikes back together. But they weren't the bikes we started with, any longer.

In fact, they weren't two bikes. It was a single bike. Sort of.

The first thing I noticed were the wheels, three across the back and one in front. The silly little banana seats were gone. In their place, in a framed cockpit with a canopy over the top, sat the cushioned parts of two old bar stools side-by-side. On the left was a set of handlebars, colorful handles still attached, bent into a U shape and mounted to the framework.

"What's that?" I pointed.

"We need to steer."

Of course we did. I kept looking. Between the seats were two levers with hand grips.

"Okay, what about those?"

Cass sat down. "This one is a hand throttle. Squeeze and press the handle down and we go faster, let go or pull it back and we slow down. The other one's the brake, and it's simple. Squeeze and we slow down."

On the floor, on both sides, were the pedals.

"We still have to pedal?" This was disappointing. After all this work, I expected miracles.

"Yes, but it doesn't do what we did."

"Huh?" She lost me, but she explained. The pedals were connected to generators. The generators were connected to batteries, hidden under the seats. She pulled a seat up and smiled, proud of her work. There had to be two dozen batteries under there, of all different size, and an octopus of wires hooking them all together.

"Why?" I waved at the different batteries.

"It's what I found." She continued to show off her creation.

At the back sat a motor she scrounged and linked to an axle with one of our bike chains, around the gearing she'd salvaged. At the ends of the axle were wheels, and the third in the center. The motor was connected to the batteries, and I finally got it. We had an electric bike. Trike. Something.

I noticed the canopy. "Wasn't that the kayak we found?"

"Uh-huh. I cut off the broken part. We don't want to get wet, do we?"

"I guess not."

After she finished we sort of stood back and looked. This was totally not a bike any longer!

"You wanna?" she said after a minute.

"Duh!"

We jumped in and buckled up. "Start pedaling."

"Why?"

"We want to keep the batteries as charged as possible."

Oh. I pedaled. After a couple minutes she pushed the throttle forward and we started creeping out of the barn, absolutely silently.

When we'd made it to the road she dared to open up the throttle a bit more. It was still raining, but we were dry and the tires held the weight. Well, we went down that country road, turned, went some more, turned again, and by then she was feeling good.

"Want to go fast?"

"Uh-huh!"

"Pedal harder! We don't want to run out of power."

I did, and so did she, and we flew down the road. The rain smacked our faces, coming up from the roadway, but we didn't care. It was too much fun.

That's probably why we didn't see the looks on the cops' faces when we passed them.

The next thing we know they pulled alongside. One of her few oversights was not installing rear-view mirrors. I glance over first, sensing their presence, and see the one in the passenger seat's pointing for us to pull over. I tap Cass's shoulder and point. She went absolutely pale before pulling on the brake and we stop.

They got out of their car and walked back, looking more amused than angry. One stopped next to me, one next to Cass, and they gave us the classic line: "License and registration, please." They had to stoop because the whole thing wasn't more than four feet tall.

We had no clue what they meant and told them so.

"Who are you?" We give our names, and they dutifully punch them into their little handhelds; I have to explain why my name didn't match my parents.

"Where did you get this car?"

Cass, indignant, said, "It's not a car, I built it with Kendra from our bikes!"

That wasn't anything they were ready to process, so they moved on.

"Where do you live?"

This threw Cass, but I'd always had a good sense of direction and distance. I pointed back, over my shoulder, and said, "That way, about eight kilometers, on County Road 5."

The one on Cass's side took off her hat and leaned under the canopy. "Well, you ought to get home. This road's a state road, and you really shouldn't be riding your, um, bike on a state road. Not in the rain."

Cass, who had figured out this hadn't been such a good idea, said, "Yes, ma'am," which I echoed.

"You sure you know how to get home?"

"I never get lost," I said. Not bragging, just fact.

They got back in their car and drove off; Cass turned us around and, much more subdued, drove us home.

By then, our parents noticed we were gone and were waiting, in force, for us to return. I think they were going to lecture us about going out in the rain on our bikes for so long, but that went out the airlock when they saw us pull up.

I was grounded for two weeks. Cass got three since it was her idea. We didn't mind too much. Grounding meant we couldn't use the bike, but we were still allowed to play together.

Her dad and my mom worked that thing over, making some tweaks to it. When we were finally allowed to have it back we found it had a nav system, better batteries (though we still had to pedal), a proper steering wheel, mirrors, lights, a windshield, all the things that would keep us safe. They told Cass how proud they were of her, and her dad specifically mentioned the seat belts. Cass blushed.

During our grounding, my dad made some quiet inquiries. He let the local police know about our new ride and figured out how to get it registered properly. From then on, whenever we saw one on our excursions, all we got was a wave. Well, except the one time with the Northern Imperium Border Patrol, but that's another story. Oh, and the time we accidentally crossed the border into Big Sky.

We spent the rest of the summer riding around. The new batteries gave us about fifty kilometers range, without charging. If we pedaled, our range was only limited to our imaginations. We explored the entire county, and most of the next county over.

It was the greatest freedom I knew until I was much, much older.

The Bikes 2

WE SPENT ALL SUMMER in that bike. Trike. Quad-rider. Whatever you want to call it.

Aiyana was the first one to drive it. Fair enough. She came up with the idea, and she built it with only minimal help from me. By minimal I mean that she did all the work and I maybe held things in place while she welded and hammered and wrenched – is that a thing?

Anyways, after a couple weeks of her doing all the driving, she let me drive. She gave me a careful course in what each pedal and lever did, then forced me to practice in the street between our homes before we went anywhere.

Boy, did I love it! Frankly, I blame her for my love of speed and cars and all that, the thrill-seeking, adrenaline-junkie stuff I've been dealing with ever since.

Right. The not-bikes.

We probably covered fifty kilometers a day, which was enough to get us into town and around before heading back home. We had fun, wandering the stores and doing some oh-so-adult shopping. At first the shopkeepers were pretty wary of us. After all, two little girls, unaccompanied? Who'd think we had any money?

Then I got the bright idea of asking my parents for money, and then things changed. *Boy*, did things change! This was probably June. I know it was early summer, because the crops were still growing, not even close to harvesting, and we were still taller than the corn. My dad gave me a twenty Daley note, and told us to have fun.

Wait, I hear you say. He gave you money and freedom to go off and do things?

Well, yeah. Dad was older, and I was his I never expected to foster a child daughter, so he was pretty relaxed about most of the things we did. Building a vehicle and driving all over the county? Piece of cake.

Like I said, this was middle-of-nowhere, Minnesota. It wasn't a poor area, but there wasn't tons of money, right? A couple five-year-olds certainly wouldn't have any money, or have the slightest idea how to spend it.

So we drove into town. I drove, actually, and Aiyana held onto the seat with white-knuckled hands. Did I mention I blame her for my addiction to speed? I had that thing full out, motors whining, and we're pedaling like crazy because otherwise we'd drain the batteries too fast, all the way into town, and I only slowed down because the local police had warned us not to go faster than any car we came across on the road.

We pulled up in front of this little restaurant and headed in, holding hands, and I said to the older woman – ha, older, she was probably twenty, but I was five! – "Can we have a table please?"

She humored me and brought us to a table.

"Do you need menus?"

I looked at Cass, who nodded.

"Yes, please."

She brings the full menus and, to her surprise, we both start reading them. Cass, I think I said, could read when she was, like, three, and I had started to read the year before to keep up with her. I could handle the menu, just about.

"I'd like a grilled cheese," I said, feeling very grown-up. "And a glass of milk."

"Can I have a Caesar salad? And water." Cass always had more mature tastes.

The waitress collects the menus with a stern look. "Okay, enough playtime."

Cass frowns at her. "What do you mean?"

"I mean, I don't mind you pretending to read the menu, or playing at ordering, but I know you don't have any money, and —"

"I do so!" I say, indignant, and pull out the bill. "See?"

Cass is even angrier. "I did not pretend!" She's as angry as only a child can be.

"Yes, you did," insists the waitress.

"I'll prove it!" says Cass. "Bring me a book!"

Smirking, the waitress goes off and comes back with a book from under the counter. Someone must have left it behind, because I don't think that most hole-in-the-wall cafes have copies of <u>Great Expectations</u> just lying around.

"If you can read this, I'll buy your lunch!" she says, and opens it at a random page.

Cass picks up the book and runs through it all perfectly. The waitress, who was peering over her shoulder, goes pale as she realizes how badly she judged Cass. After a minute, Cass closed the book and looked up at the waitress, innocence personified. "Is that enough?"

"Uh, um, yes, that's plenty, yes."

"I'll have a milkshake, too. Strawberry."

"Me too!" I added. "Chocolate."

We didn't make a friend then, but we got our lunch and never had a problem at another shop in town. Word got around quick. Cass even insisted we tip her; I told you she was a genius.

Well, I seem to have rambled for a while, but I have one more story you need about that summer: the border-crossing incident.

The Bikes 3

AFTER THE INCIDENT at the café, we didn't have any issues in town with the shops. Looking back, it might have made us a little bit overconfident.

Key West was, is, a real nothing town. It didn't take long for us to get bored with the shops and downtown and what little there was to see, but we didn't have a problem. The batteries in Aiyana's bodged-together transport were good for about fifty kilometers on their own, if she was driving. If I drove, we'd get about twenty, but I was always more aggressive than her.

With the pedals and our efforts we had effectively unlimited range, and it wasn't long before we started going farther and farther afield. We went to Bygland; no, it's not pronounced big-land but by-glend, and yes, it's a real place. We went to Fisher, and Euclid, and Wylie and Agnus and Tabor and Warren, but they were all pretty similar to our hometown: wide spots in the road.

We didn't want to go to Grand Forks. Well, we did, but we knew we wouldn't be allowed. After all, Grand Forks was The Big City in the area, the place we all went for special things and occasions, all the shopping we couldn't do anywhere locally but didn't want to get over the net. It was big and noisy and covered with permacrete and steel, which took away its charms. Neither

Cass or I wanted to drive in it in our homebuilt ride, and we just didn't want to in any case.

We were still bored with the little towns, though, so one day we asked if we could go to Crookston, which was only about thirty kilometers away. It was the county seat, a real city to us girls, and we were shocked when our parents all agreed! Before they could change their minds, we were off.

Cass had the usual twenty her dad gave her, plus what she'd saved up from our earlier adventures. She was always more frugal than me, thinking about rainy days.

"It rains all the time!" I had said; I didn't get the expression.

"Not that kind, I think," she said, but she didn't explain any more. She believed, and understood, that saving a few daleys was a good idea.

I filched a fifty daley bill from my mom's secret hiding place. Why she thought it was secret, I don't know; Dad and I both knew about it. Anyhow, there was more money in there than I'd seen in one place before, so I figured she wouldn't miss the fifty.

I was right, actually, but that was the least of our issues before the day was done.

Crookston was nice. Old-fashioned, like, pre-20th Century old-fashioned. We parked the bike, took the wheel – didn't I mention that?

There wasn't an ignition, like a car. No, the bike was always on, ready to go. If you could fit, you could go. Aiyana's dad pointed that little flaw out to us when we started going into town, and since we didn't want to walk home we listened to what he said. He rigged it so the steering wheel came off by pulling a single pin, and made us promise to take it with us whenever we parked. We always did.

There we were, though, walking around with a wheel in my backpack, and having a blast. We felt very grown-up, and oh, was it fun! We got some funny looks, but there were enough people like us, kids, I mean, that we didn't stand out too much.

After we had lunch, which she paid for, we went shopping. I found a flower I knew my mom would love, so I got that. Aiyana found a pile of books which cost less than my flower did, but I still had enough out of that fifty to get them for her and ice cream, too. We put everything in the bike then wandered some more.

At about three we decided it was time to go home. We still had a few hours of daylight, but there were always more chores for us when we got home, plus dinner, and we wanted to look at our treasures before bed.

You know, now that I'm thinking about it, I don't get how that worked. Chores, that is. See, we had to do our chores before we could go play. Didn't finish, didn't get to go. Simple. But there were always more chores later.

Huh.

Wonder why I never noticed this before.

Back to the story. Where was I?

Oh, yes. Going home to do chores.

Well, we took the wrong road. We were supposed to take Imperial Highway 2, and we took Province Road 9.

Okay, okay. Confession time: I was driving, so *I* took the wrong road. Hey, it's an easy mistake to make, they converge in the center of downtown, they both head west, it's just IH2 bends north and brings us towards 350 and home. PR9 doesn't bend. Usually, we didn't have any problem with it, but I was distracted. We'd had a big day, and we were laughing and talking, and I flat-out missed the turn.

Well, I'm driving along, going almost as fast as the occasional car, when Cass says, "Kendra?"

"Yeah?"

"I think we're lost."

"No, we're not lost!" I was utterly sure of this. Besides my generally excellent sense of direction, this was a road we'd taken lots of times with our parents. Plus, we had the old satnav, but you know something? Truth be told, I hadn't looked at it even once, because this was old hat. I mean, doesn't every five-year-old know how to drive around their county?

"I think we are." She was insistent, and she tapped at the nav. "See?"

"No, I can't, I'm not supposed to take my eyes off the road!" Which was true, if unfair to bring up. After all, I spent enough time looking at scenery. I could have looked, but I had a creeping sensation that she was right and I didn't want to be proven wrong.

About then we crossed a river, zipping over a big bridge, and I know she's right. We went over all sorts of bridges and creeks, but there weren't any big rivers, and this one was.

"Maybe you're right." It hurt to say it, but I could give in gracefully. Almost gracefully. I slow down. "Can you get us home?"

She starts fiddling with the nav, and that's when I notice flashing lights.

No problem. Most of the cops knew us by now, but there were always occasional new ones. I knew the drill, and pulled off the road.

"Hello," I said when I could see legs.

"Do you know where you are?" says a voice.

"Not really, but we're working on it!" I say.

"You're in Big Sky."

Um. What?

"Huh?"

"Please step out of the, uh, vehicle."

I get out and I notice the uniform is different from the ones I'm used to seeing. And isn't it telling that I knew what the police uniforms should have looked like? A little disconcerting, in retrospect.

"Where do you live?"

"Key West." I knew this part.

"Do you have ID?" he says. Gently, I have to admit. I don't think he was expecting a little blonde girl to be driving on a highway.

"No," I say. "But you can call our parents."

"We'll get to that. Why did you cross the border?"

"Huh?" I was not at my finest.

He points behind us. "The bridge back there is the border between the Imperium and Big Sky. You're not supposed to cross without permission."

"Nobody stopped us!" I protested. Which was true, but what I didn't know is all the cars and hovercars and aircars and all the vehicles that, you know, normal people had were equipped with transponders. The signals were picked up automatically and registered.

We didn't have a transponder. Nobody thought we'd be crossing the border.

Whoops.

"Why are you in Big Sky?" he asks again.

"We got lost. I got lost," I correct, owning it.

He was remarkably calm about a child driving.

"Do you need help getting home?"

Cass speaks up and says, "No, I have it figured out now." I think he forgot she was in there because he jumps, then leans down and looks in to see her smiling. That smile works on anyone, and it worked on him.

"Okay, I think I can let, wait."

He leans back down and looks behind the seat.

"What's that?" He points to the plant.

"It's a present for my Mama," I say.

"Do you know what kind of plant it is?"

"No, just that it's pretty."

This was the wrong answer, because he gets all stern. "Big Sky has strict laws about importing plants."

"But I'm not importing it!" I didn't know what importing was, but I was certain I didn't do it.

"Miss, bringing a plant into Big Sky without permission isn't allowed. I'm sorry, but you're in big trouble."

Now, I don't know quite what's going on, but if I'm in trouble I'm going down swinging. "I have my receipt!" I say, and dig for it. "Here!" I shove it in his hands.

He takes it and looks, finding the plant on it. "I'll have to check, but you're really not supposed to bring those into Big Sky."

I'm angry and frustrated and burst out with, "I didn't know I was in your stupid country!"

Wrong answer. Now he's not happy at all, and he makes us get out and sit in the back of his smelly car while he runs scans on us, checks it out, and calls our parents. Forty of the longest minutes of my life later, my dad pulls up and he and Cass's mom get out of his old truck. They talk to the border officer and calm him down.

The officer opens the door and my dad pokes his head in.

"Not one word, Kendra Marissa. Not one."

For once, I listen.

They load the bike into the back of the truck, thank the officer, and strap us in.

I think I cried the whole way home. Didn't do me any good. I was still grounded for the rest of the week. Cass got off easy, since she wasn't driving, and was allowed to come over and hang out with me. I suppose it wasn't all bad, then.

And my mom got her plant.

It was an Amazon Lily. I looked it up the other day, and it's still illegal in Big Sky. No clue why.

School Days 2

EVENTUALLY, OF COURSE, summer ended as it always does, and it ended the exact same way: too soon. It was time to go back to school, and we were together again in First Grade.

I have to back up to give you some context.

The town we lived in was too small to have its own school. There weren't enough kids to support a school, not even an elementary school. We could have stayed home and done school remotely, but both our families wanted us to get to meet other kids. After all, she and I had been virtually inseparable since forever, so having other friends was probably important to them. Maybe. Of course, I'm just guessing, but as a parent myself now, I think I have a pretty good take.

The regional school had students from all the surrounding towns and was located in Fisher. Most towns had a couple dozen students, but Key West was so small there were only four of us: Cass, me, her brother, and another kid named Marie.

It was close to us, relatively speaking, about eighteen kilometers, right down Imperial Highway2. We, *I*, argued we should be allowed to drive there, and I think I would have gotten my way except the school didn't have any provisions in the rules for students driving themselves. It was an elementary school, after all. We could be taken by our parents, we could be picked up by a bus, or if we lived in Fisher we could walk.

Well, we couldn't walk. Oh, at the beginning of the year it wouldn't be bad, just tedious, but neither of us wanted to think about walking in the winter. You know. October.

None of our parents wanted to drive.

The bus it was.

I don't know how they decided the routes; it's one of those bureaucratic mysteries of life. But it ended up on our route we were the second and third people picked up. We always crowded Shawn out of the way, teaming up on him to keep him behind us.

The first pick up? A boy named Joe DeLory, who we knew slightly. He was in our kindergarten class the previous year, but he liked to hang out with the boys, you know? It probably didn't help that Cass was taller than him, but then again, she was taller than everyone except the teacher.

Right, so Joe was on first; he lived outside Key West by a few kilometers. Then the bus would go and pick up another fifteen kids, starting with Marie, going out to Sullivan before circling North to Tabor, Sherack, and Keystone before heading to the school. In all, it was about a seventy minute ride for us, which meant we were on the bus from 7:08 (yes, I remember precisely) so we'd be to school in time for the 8:30am start.

The plus side is it gave us plenty of time to play and have fun with the other kids. We got to know them all, of course, and since we were early on/late off, we had seniority on the bus. Which meant, silly as it sounds, that the other kids wanted to hang with us simply because we were there first.

After about a week of getting to know our busmates, we're riding home one day and we decide it would be a good idea to start playing tag on the bus.

Wait.

I have to explain about our buses, don't I?

Well, they're still yellow. Somehow that's stayed the official bus color, even by the late 21st Century, but the design changed.

See, by the middle of the century the profession of bus driver had gotten so hazardous the entire design was re-thought to isolate the driver from the students. Now, you might think it foolish with five- and six-year-olds, but the design was for *all* buses, no matter who was using them. It was too much of a challenge, I guess, to have a design for the kids who weren't going to be a threat and another for bigger, more risky kids.

It coincided with the transition to all-electric and fuel cell vehicles, marking a major opportunity. The manufacturers took it. When I grew up, we had a bus with the driver up front, in a totally isolated cab. It didn't even have a door to get from the cab into the seating area. If the driver needed to do that, they had to stop, get out, and come around to one of the doors.

There was a seat up front which was armored, in case the school thought they needed an active guard presence.

We didn't have a guard.

Behind it you had all the seats, and they weren't benches like you have now, they were proper, individual seats. See, that's how they made them interchangeable; you just swapped seats in and out. Smaller kids, smaller seats, ones designed for the appropriate weights and heights. Bigger kids, bigger seats.

The overall design ended up with two rows of seats and a wide passage between them, and each row had two seats on each side of the passage. Got it?

Like I was saying, we were playing tag, and having a blast. It was a beautiful day and recess just wasn't long enough, so we all had way too much energy. I was it and I was chasing after Cass.

Well, duh. Who else would I chase?

All the other kids figured out what I'm doing, and they decided to protect her by getting in my way. I didn't want to tag them, I wanted to tag Cass, so when one got in my way I'd have to slow down and go around them, trying not to touch them. It was fun for a while, but eventually I got frustrated. I went to my seat and picked up my backpack, then used it to push them out of the way. I wasn't touching them, so they couldn't say they were it, right?

Cass saw me coming, squeaked, and dove under the seats to hide.

It didn't work. I finally got through all the interference and tagged her.

"You're it!" I crowed.

"You cheated!"

"Did not!"

"Did too!"

"They were in my way!"

"So?"

"So? What do you mean, so?"

"You could have tagged them!"

"I wanted to tag you, and I did. You're it!"

At this she started to sniffle.

"I didn't want to be it!"

"That's the game, silly!"

The sniffling grew louder.

"Aw, come on, Cass," I said. I was getting uncomfortable. Her unhappy made me unhappy.

"You…" Sniffle. "Cheated!" Sniffle.

She was wiggling her way out now, going forward, and every other kid on the bus was watching. Drama is always fascinating, isn't it, especially when it happens to someone else?

"I didn't cheat," I repeated, but it sounded weak to my ears.

"Cheater!" she said, with another sniff. She was out from under, now, on the other side of the seats from me.

"Am not!" I said, and I plopped into the seat behind her. I crossed my arms on my chest and dropped my chin, ready to do a full pout.

"You are too!" said Aiyana.

By now I had my eyes closed, trying to fight back tears and failing, which meant I totally missed what was going on around me. I did notice it was real quiet, but I didn't particularly think anything of it.

Then I felt a hand on my arm, and Aiyana was kissing my forehead. My eyes flew open and I saw her looking at me, those big blue eyes staring right into mine.

She and I had kissed. It was natural as breathing for us to trade a kiss and a hug first thing in the morning, or last thing before going home. But this was the first time she kissed me as anything other than a greeting.

"You okay?" she said.

"I didn't cheat!" I answered, still upset.

"I know. I was mad. I'm sorry."

"You are?"

"Uh-huh."

She kissed me, on the lips this time, and then leaned away.

"Oh, yeah. You're it."

And with a squeal of joy she dashed away.

I just sat there for a moment trying to process it all, then I was after her again, with the other kids saying, 'Let Kendra catch her girlfriend!'

Which I did. Aiyana then tagged another kid, and the game moved on, but for the rest of the year we always had seats saved for us together. It was a warm feeling, having someone outside our immediate families recognize what we had, even if we didn't yet have a clue what it was or could be.

We were just better together.

Our Birthday

THAT WAS THE YEAR WE turned six.

You know, I've always wondered what would have happened if my host mother hadn't gotten into that accident.

Accident? Yes; Jane and Hal, Mama and Dad, were my foster parents. My host mother had a serious accident before I was born, so I was delivered by Caesarian on the way to the hospital. My expected arrival date was supposed to be December 5th. Given my actual birth weight and size – 39 centimeters, 2.1 kilograms – I would have been about 55-57 centimeters and 3.5 kilograms if I'd gone to term, while Cass was 54 centimeters and 3.2 kilograms at birth. Now, I know premature babies are supposed to catch up to full-term babies by the time they're two or so, but I have to wonder. Would I have been as tall as Cass? She's only a few centimeters taller than I am now. Okay, okay. Twelve centimeters, if you want to get picky about it.

In any case, we were six that year, and she and I got into a hell of a fight.

Our birthdays are three weeks apart, exactly. In 2086, our actual birthdays were on Mondays, which sucked, because it was a school day and we couldn't have our parties on our actual birthdays. But it was fun, because it was a school day and everyone in our class made a fuss over each of us on our day. I guess it wasn't all bad.

Our parents decided we'd have a joint birthday. I suspect it was mostly my parents; they'd already done the whole bring up children thing by the time I stumbled into their lives. I knew they loved me, but they didn't always have time for me. Or patience. Or energy, for that matter. I think they found the idea of a bunch of six-year-olds running around the house a bit intimidating.

The date they settled on was October 5, the Saturday closest to the middle. Invitations were duly sent, hand-delivered by us on the bus and in the school, and Cass's folks started to prepare for a horde of schoolchildren to descend on their home.

We helped, mostly by staying out of the way, but we were excited. It was the first joint birthday, and we were giddy with the idea we'd be celebrating together. It seemed perfectly natural, too, a "Why haven't we done this before?" moment. We did everything else together, after all. Why not this?

Finally, finally, it was the morning of the party, and we got exiled to my house for the surprise preparations. We had strict instructions not to get dirty, as we'd been bathed and dressed nicely. At least as nicely as we'd stand it, which meant clean clothes which didn't have any visible tears or stains. Maybe they were low standards, but we were rough on clothing, especially me. There was never a nail I couldn't find!

We did our best, but as you might guess we didn't succeed.

We were running around the yard. We were kids, and we'd been told we couldn't take the bike, so, running. It was Minnesota, in early fall, one of those beautiful days where the temperature spiked up to about 30 and it was sunny and beautiful. We kicked off our shoes and socks and were having a blast.

Until Cass stepped in the cow droppings.

She didn't just step in them; she went full-on up to her ankle in one, and then skidded and fell.

It was impressive, in a smelly, disgusting sort of way.

I don't know quite how I did it but I managed to avoid the splatter and come to a stop.

"You okay?"

She nodded. "Uh-huh. But it stinks!"

I reached out to pull her up, then wrinkled my nose. "You're right."

I think that's when she realized what had happened, and processed through the consequences.

"Oh no!" she wailed.

I wasn't as quick to figure it out, but I knew she was hurting. "What's wrong?"

"My clothes!"

Then it hit me, too. Oh crap.

"It's all your fault!" she yelled.

"My fault?"

"If you weren't chasing me I wouldn't have fallen!"

Well, her logic was sound, but I wasn't going to admit it.

"If you weren't so clumsy you wouldn't have stepped in the cow pie!" Yes. That's what I called them.

"You ruined my clothes!"

"Did not! You fell!"

"Because you were chasing me!"

More logic, but I had a comeback. "Because you were running!" I thought I had her there.

"Dummy!"

This was new, and low. We both knew that Cass was smarter than me. I wasn't stupid, by any means, but she was, is, so smart she simply doesn't compare to most people. We never discussed it. It was one of the things she did well, or better than me, just like I could do things better than her.

"Am not!" Hardly a blistering retort.

"Are too!"

Then she scooped up a handful of the pie and flung it at me!

I dodged, but the second handful was aimed where she figured I'd duck and it hit me squarely in the chest. Of course, at that point there was nothing for it but to jump on her and try to get her to stop, since she had all the ammo.

The fact we were rolling around on a rapidly-flattening cow pie was totally lost on us, as we both tried to pound the hell out of the other.

It was our first real fight, in the sort of "I'm mad and I'm going to do my best to hurt you" way. Neither of us knew what we were doing, not really, though Aiyana did have an advantage: her older brother. Which meant she had the equivalent of a graduate course in torment. What saved me was she hadn't yet completely developed the cool head in a crisis she has today. She got mad and she forgot a bunch of what she wanted to do to me, in other words.

She still thumped me good. Have I mentioned she's always been taller? Probably. She ended up straddling my middle, doing her best to hit my head, but I was smart enough to bring my arms up and block most of them while yelling as loudly as I could.

Her mom came running out and screeched to a halt when she caught sight of us. I can only imagine the scene, from her perspective: her daughter, red hair all wild and frizzed out, covered with cow poo from nose to toes, sitting on top of her best friend, and whaling away with both fists. Said best friend, yours truly, equally covered in lovely cow by-products and screaming mostly incoherently for help.

Honestly, if it was me, I might have grabbed a hose. We were both messy and smelly and thoroughly disreputable. Worse, the party was supposed to be starting in about ten minutes.

I found out later, much later, years later, that while she was staring at us in horror the first guest arrived.

But no, no hose, just a yelp of, "Aiyana!"

I swear Cass levitated, she was off me so fast. Then I was up, too. We're both standing there with hang-dog looks on our faces, though not looking at each other, and her mom's face is mortified. That might have gone on for hours, but then a door slammed and it broke the spell.

"Aiyana Rosewind Cassidy! March yourself, no." She rethought what she was going to say. "You and Kendra go over to her house and bathe. I don't know what this was about, and I don't care right now. We'll discuss it later, you can be sure." That was a promise of certain doom.

"I don't wanna go to her house," Cass muttered, loudly enough for me to hear but not her mom.

"I don't want your stinky butt in my house," I said, just as quietly.

Her mom had better ears than we thought. Before we could escalate, she said, "I don't care what either of you want. Unless you want me to call off your party you're going to get cleaned up at Kendra's house!"

"Yes, Mom," Cass said.

"Yes, ma'am," I said simultaneously.

We trudged the couple hundred meters that separated our homes, miserable and sullen and wrapped in our own thoughts. When we finally made it, several lifetimes later, Dad was standing outside, waiting for us. I had the wisdom not to speak.

"Clothes off. I don't know whether to burn them or bury them," he said, half-joking. We dropped the smelly things on the grass and followed him into the house to the downstairs bathroom. A bath was already filling.

Have I mentioned my Dad was a really smart guy? I mean, yeah, he was a retired diplomat, but that's nothing. He was *smart*.

He had a *bubble bath* running.

Now, I didn't ask whether or what he'd heard, then or later. Based on the bubble bath? He must have been told something about what happened, and the mood we both seemed to be in.

Bubbles always made everything better!

By the time we were in the bath for two minutes, we were giggling and splashing each other, mad forgotten.

In ten minutes we were clean and didn't smell like cow. In fifteen we were dried off and dressed and headed back, hand-in-hand. They weren't the planned party clothes, but at least we were dressed and unsmelly.

Oh, where did Cass get the clothes? She and I spent so much time at each other's home that our parents just kept some portion of our wardrobes at the other house. She didn't have the selection she'd have at home, but it was enough so we were both smiling and happy with how we looked, and that's how we ended up getting to our first joint birthday party fashionably late.

Never did see those outfits again, now I think of it.

Helloween

NO, THAT'S NOT A TYPO or misspelling.

We both loved dressing up and pretending. My folks had all the clothes from their older children, mostly because Dad was a bit of a hoarder. I know, you wouldn't expect that from a diplomat, right?

Actually, being a diplomat is perfect for being a hoarder. You go to all these places and can ship stuff back on the government's dime, plus maybe get them at a way better price. Then you have your home, so you have a place to put all the artwork and treasures you collect. If you're a really successful diplomat, who can afford a big house, well, you have room for *lots* of stuff!

Dad was a really successful diplomat, so much so he was being called on for consultation even though he'd officially retired three years before I was born.

I seem to have misplaced my train of thought.

Clothes!

All the clothes my semi-siblings had, at least everything which was in good shape, was stashed away somewhere in the home. Dad, like I said, was a bit of a hoarder. Mom was organized and knew where to find things. When I came along, I had pretty much all the clothes I would ever need, if a few decades out of date.

You know, now I'm thinking of it, I wonder if my lifelong fascination with the early part of the 21st Century came from Dad's trinkets?

Aiyana dipped into my clothes stash pretty liberally, too. Like I said last time, we each had clothes over at the other's house, but then we'd be doing something and Aiyana would see something she liked and borrow it and it would go home with her.

So we played dress-up, and most of the time it was just for us, for fun, but October was big. October was Halloween, and October meant we could walk around in our costumes and pretend to be people. Us being who we were, and our parents having decided to roll with it rather than try to fight it, we started dressing up about the middle of September and went right through until sometime in November. Not only that but we'd also wear our outfits *everywhere*.

We had fun.

We did all the boring typical schoolkid stuff: police and firefighters, doctors, teachers, farmers, that sort. We also did more out-there outfits. I raided Dad's clothes, and played at being a politician and a soldier and, of course, a diplomat. Digging deeper, we found old clothes and suddenly we were rebels from the Second Civil War. Then we got creative. I asked Mama if I could use, alter, some of the clothes, so over the course of a week she went through every scrap and made a pile of clothes we could cut to pieces.

One Thursday Cass and I went to school as bellydancers. We hadn't the slightest clue what the story was or why it was a thing, but we loved the veils and the filmy skirts we made out of something we found. And the cymbals on the fingers...! By the end of the day we had three other girls, and two boys, following us around and trying to do the same wiggles we did!

But Halloween was coming, and we really wanted to do something special.

Now, by '86 I was well into my fandoms, and I was watching all the television and movies I could get my hands on. Cass watched them too, but not as often and not nearly with my obsession over the details. One show we enjoyed was called <u>Buffy the Vampire Slayer</u>. I mean, what little girl didn't want to kick monster butt?

So we decided we were going to be Willow and Buffy.

The clothes weren't tough, since it was just teenager clothes.

Props were easy too. Stakes? Simple. Crosses? Well, we didn't have any, but we could get some. Dad even had an old crossbow he let me borrow, but didn't give me any quarrels, and he took the string so I couldn't improvise anything. Probably a smart move.

Becoming the characters? Tougher, but we had seen all of the first three seasons by then and could manage.

Practicing the martial arts? Yeah, that was the challenge.

We watched and watched and watched until we felt we had a certain scene down, then we'd practice the moves as best we could figure out. Then another, and another. Usually Cass would be Giles or the vampire or whoever Buffy was trying to slay while I did my moves, and then we'd trade places. Of course, usually Willow wasn't kicking butt as much as being rescued, but she had her moments, and we took advantage of that.

Finally it's the week before Halloween, and we decided we were going to be Buffy and Willow all day, every day, until Halloween night. We insisted our parents call us by the right names, dressed like Buffy and Willow.

In retrospect Cass got the better end of the deal. I don't know if you know <u>Buffy</u> at all, but the main character often dressed in a blouse and short skirt, while Willow was dressed more warmly. This is *not* a minor consideration in Minnesota in October!

We boarded the bus to go to school. As everyone else gets on, we tell them to call me Buffy and her Willow. By the time we're at school, everyone's got it. We were the Big Kids on the Bus, after all, and by the end of the day everyone in school picked up on it.

The teachers were a little bit pickier, but eventually relented.

Then we had to explain to everyone who we were, and that led to me showing them an episode. I was pleased as you could possibly imagine; after all, nobody knew about <u>Buffy</u> until I brought her into school!

That was a Tuesday.

On Thursday, the first vampire showed up.

I guess it was inevitable, right? After all, I was the Slayer, but the existence of a Slayer implies creatures to slay, i.e. vampires. The kid did a pretty good job with the makeup, too.

Friday there was a whole pack of them. We had lots of fun, pretending to fight and hide and run around.

We didn't do much over the weekend, but the rest of the school did, because come Monday we had pretty well managed to transform our little school into Sunnydale. There were werewolves and vampires and creatures that went bump in the night, and even a couple of the teachers got into the act as Principal Snyder and Giles and Ms. Calendar.

Tuesday was so much fun! One girl played Cordelia and another boy was Angel, and even though I didn't like him I had to pretend to. We even a Xander. We got into staged fights with the vampires and werewolves and dutifully kicked their first-grade behinds.

Then Wednesday happened.

I guess we did too good a job kicking butt. We went out for recess and separated to play. When we went back inside I looked around but no Cass. I asked the teacher, Mr. Tamba, and he said he hadn't seen her come in either.

Then there's a knock on the door.

Mr. Temba opens the door and all there is is a note stuck to it. Written in a 6-year-old scrawl is *Send Buffy or Willow dies – the Master*

We think it's all a game, and Mr. Temba was one of the more chill teachers. He lets me leave. I walk down the hallway, wondering what to do next since there weren't any directions on the note. Then these hands grab me and pull a bag over my head and I'm kicking and swinging but I didn't manage to connect, though I hold onto my backpack.

A couple minutes later I hear a door close and the bag is pulled off my head. It looks like we're in one of the gym supply closets.

"Kendra!"

I whirl and there's Cass, held by a bunch of kids who didn't look really happy; she must have fought them hard because she's got a hell of a shiner coming on and her hair's mussed.

"What's going on?" I yell, not caring it's the middle of the day and we're in school.

"You have incon- in- made me mad!" says one kid from the back. He's dressed in black pleather and has something on his head which kinda makes him look bald, so I'm guessing he's playing the Master. He doesn't really have the menace, and my mad's up, so I'm not exactly backing down.

"Let her go!" I demand.

"No. I have read the prophecy, and you must both die."

Then Cass screams; one of the brothers ugly must have pulled her wrong.

I lose it.

You know all those moves I practiced, based on watching the show over and over? Turns out I wasn't so far off, because I start spinning at them and kicking and punching like nobody's business.

I'm sure some of the kids still thought we were playing, but I wasn't, not any more.

One grabbed my hair and pulled; I had long hair as a little girl, it wasn't until I got away from home that I went to my favorite pixie cut. This kid grabbed, and it hurt, so now I'm personally angry and not just defending Cass.

I pushed backwards into him, using the pull for an extra boost, and slam him into the wall.

One down.

Two more rush at me and all I do is step to the side. They slam into the same wall.

Three down.

The kid playing the Master forgets he's supposed to send his minions and runs towards me. I brace against the wall with one foot and kick up between his legs.

Four down.

There are three kids left holding onto Cass, who's still screaming, but they're not letting go.

That's where it all sort of goes sideways.

I kinda forget I wasn't *actually* Buffy, and these aren't *actually* vampires.

Remember, we made these costumes to be as show-accurate as we could make them, so Willow had her spelling stuff, and I had my Slaying equipment. I pull a stake out from behind my back and charge at them.

Two see the crazy in my eyes and let go, putting Cass between me and them, but the third is still holding on to one arm and yelling at me to stop or she'll hurt her.

I swing the stake at her and it penetrates her upper arm.

Suddenly there's blood everywhere and she's on the ground screaming too, Cass is sobbing, and everyone who could move is out of there.

Finally a teacher reacts to the noise. She came in and this is what she sees:

Two boys and a girl in more-or-less of a heap against one wall.

A third boy writhing on the ground, clutching his groin.

A second girl on the ground with a bloody stake through her upper arm.

And me, on the ground, rocking and holding Cass and telling her that it was all over and I saved her and she was safe now. Cass, meanwhile, isn't doing much more than whimpering.

That was the end of any learning for the day for all of us. First they got the stake out and wrapped Lyssa's arm to stop the bleeding. Then they were waking the ones who were knocked out, and convincing the Master, Jeremy, he was going to live.

Meanwhile the principal squatted down and was trying to talk to me. I don't remember particularly what I said, but I suspect I wasn't overly coherent.

Cass, though, was surprisingly eloquent once she'd calmed down. She explained that they'd come to her at recess and convinced her they were going to play a fun game, called Buffy Rescues Willow, and so she went with them. She didn't know they were going to kidnap me, or hold her so tightly, or actually try to hurt me.

The clincher, the thing that got me out of trouble, was the note that Mr. Temba wisely held onto. In light of what they wrote, the principal decided I was justified in what I did. Nobody ended up in trouble, though costume-wearing was reduced to only the day of Halloween from then on.

Funnily enough, Lyssa and I went on to be good friends all the rest of school. She never held a grudge, once I promised to teach her the moves I used. We even went on a couple double dates with Cass and one of her boyfriends in high school, and eventually she came to work with me in the Federation. But that's another story.

Winter Travels

MY PARENTS TRAVELED a bunch, but they never took me.

I don't know if it was because they were older and didn't feel they were up to taking care of me when I was little, or if they were simply sick of the hassles dragging a child around with them created. Whatever their reason, we never went farther than Grand Forks on any kind of regular basis, and all my semi-siblings and their children would come to Key West to visit.

Boring!

Every few months, they'd disappear for a weekend, or maybe a week.

Me?

I'd be shipped over to Aiyana's and we'd have an extended sleepover. It was a blast for me, for us, because Cass had her own room, and we'd stay up late and play and giggle and laugh. Sometimes, before I learned how, she'd read to me. I introduced her to some of the shows and movies I was already getting into, but her interest was always polite, not over the top like me.

Huh? Oh, no, she never got dropped with us. Well, once, but that was for a funeral, a friend of her parents, not family. We did sleepovers, of course; what kids don't? They were run-of-the-mill sleepovers, though, just a single night. But her parents, when they did travel, always took Cass with them, along with her brother the snot. They never went out of the country; I think I've mentioned before why not.

In case I didn't, well, it's not a pretty story, and tells you a bit about the country I lived in. See, when they were in college, her folks were involved in all sorts of protests and demonstrations against the Northern Imperium government, and the Daley Dynasty in particular.

I have to back up again. So much of this is just stuff I grew up with and absorbed through my skin. Thinking about it isn't as easy as you might belive.

The Daley Dynasty has ruled the Imperium since its founding in 2040; at times, it's been a tight grip, and at other times they've loosened it. There's a constitution and freedom of speech is officially guaranteed, but like most things in the Imperium it all depends on the whim of the Imperial Hand, currently His Benevolence Richard VIII, and at the time Her Benevolence Richard IV. Yes, *her* Benevolence. A quirk of the dynasty is their reigning name has to be Richard, no matter the sex of the ruler.

One of the things the Imperial Internal Affairs Bureau did, and still does, is monitor the social media of the current crop of young idiots. Zeus love them, social media has to be the best tool for control every created! Got an unpopular opinion? Flood the channels with bots that will spew your line until it's accepted as truth. Want to track down the dissidents? Who needs spies and espionage when college students are going to put everything on the 'net? Political leanings? *Hello*, have you seen them?

In any case, the IAB watches college students in particular and has for decades. Aiyana's parents were passionate and vocal about their opposition to the Daleys and Imperial policies. It didn't get them in trouble, though; not directly. Like I said, Free Speech is officially a thing.

What it did do was put them both on the untrustworthy and to be watched lists. It also got their travel privileges revoked. Oh, they could get passports, but they were only valid for travel at the sufferance of the Imperium Border Control agents. They learned this fact when they tried to get to the New Confederacy for their honeymoon and were denied permission to exit.

Now, the Imperium's a pretty big place, comprising the former states of Minnesota, Illinois, Michigan, and Wisconsin. It's pretty, with lots of woods and lakes to explore, but it's all the same climate, more or less. If you're in the Imperium in winter, you're gonna be cold. If you want warm, you'd better bundle up. I mean, sure, Chicago is a neat city, but you can only walk around downtown so many times.

Okay, got the picture? My parents went places, and Cass's didn't.

After our little Helloween escapade, life was quiet for a few weeks. The annual Harvest Festival came and went. We kids didn't care about the origins of the Festival. All that mattered was we got a half-week off school. Over the weekend, when both families gathered for the big supper, my parents said they had an announcement.

After the rooba-rooba quieted down, Dad cleared his throat. Over the next few minutes, he explained. It seemed that Dad pulled some strings and got the travel ban lifted on the

Cassidys. As a result, over the Winter Solstice break, and a bit more, we'd all be going to Florida in the New Confederacy.

Cass and I nearly bounced out of our chairs in our eagerness to hug him, but he held us back. I was afraid for a second he was going to say something like, "Not you, Kendra," but he had this big smile on his face.

"We're going to take you three to DisneyWorld."

Damn. Shawn too. That was the one thing which could put a damper on my enthusiasm.

Wait. Three? Mama and Dad was two, plus Cass and me and the jerk was five, plus Tammie and Charles was seven. I could count really well, and it didn't add up. "Dad? Three?"

"Tammie and Charles are going to get their honeymoon, finally –"

Which meant nothing to me, being six.

"—in Key West."

"But we live in Key West!"

Cass elbowed me and said, "No, silly, the island! Can we go too?"

Her dad looked at her and said, "No, sweetie."

Cass started to pout. I heard Dad, leaning over Charles, whispering, "Maybe we can do something at the end; we have plenty of time to do everything. We'll work it out."

I know nobody else heard it, which surprised me. Even when I was little my peculiar genetic inheritance was evident if you knew what to look for. All I knew is I could hear things others couldn't, and I definitely heard that and nobody else did.

Cass moved on from her incipient pout. "Key West is pretty, but what's DisneyWorld?"

Yeah, she asked that question.

Oh boy.

Of course, I didn't know, either, not really, but I knew what Disney was and had all sorts of visions in my head.

Little did I know...

How Much Trouble Can They Get Into?

CASS'S DAD TOLD HER what DisneyWorld was, and she was even more excited than before.

Me?

I was over the moon happy. Not only was I finally getting to come along, but I would be sharing it with my best friend!

The adults made the smart decision and totally excluded us kids from the planning. Completely. At least after the first announcement.

Oh, they told us what was happening, about once a week. Then Cass would drag me off and we'd spend the next week researching and doing virtual tours and all that good stuff.

I mentioned she's a frakking genius, right?

The first week, all we did was search for information on Disney, and boy were we psyched! Many of my favorite movies tied back to it, so I was pointing at the screens and squealing with every new image. We were so excited, we even let Shawn look in on what we were doing. Cass had a prickly relationship with him, but I thought he was cute, so I talked her into letting him in. Occasionally.

It kept getting better the more we looked. There were full-VR recordings of all the rides, so we plotted and planned what we were going to do and how many times we were going to do them.

By the middle of December, I think everyone at school was wishing we'd disappear, or at least shut up. It was 24/7 trip talk, and *the* topic of conversation with us. It was okay, because even when nobody would listen to us we had each other.

The first fly in the ointment? The passport trip.

We all had to go to Duluth to get passports and exit visas. Why Duluth?

Because the Imperium is stupidly centralized and they are past masters at erecting bureaucratic obstacles to prevent their citizens from doing things which are legal but the Imperium frowns on. One of those is getting a passport. They know they're not the friendliest country on the continent, and so they don't want their citizens traveling outside and seeing just how badly off they are in the Imperium. Some travel is a necessity, of course, and freedom of movement is guaranteed by the Constitution, but there's nothing to stop them from making it a bitch to do.

So they do.

The passport itself is easy to get. You travel to the office, fill out a form, do some biometric identification, pay your money, and in about a day you get notified you have a travel document headed your way. Or you can wait at the office, pay a little extra, and get it more or less immediately, if you're going to be using it and don't want to make two trips. That's the option our folks decided to take, and that's where the nightmare *really* got going.

The best way to get there would have been to head over to Grand Forks and catch a jump over to Duluth. Up, over, down, be there in about thirty minutes from boarding to debarking. Unfortunately, as we discovered, Big Sky doesn't look kindly at people crossing their borders without permission, and Cass's parents only had permission for the single trip to Key West via Big Sky. Any other trip was right out.

Even if Big Sky would allow them in, the Customs and Border Inspection on arriving in Duluth was a major problem. If they couldn't leave the Imperium, how could they enter it? On top of that, none of us kids had any proof of citizen ship that the CBI would accept. Without proof of our Imperial citizenship, there would have been problems. Big problems. Like, "How do you feel about prison food?" problems. Oh, Dad might have gotten off, with his diplomatic background, but Cass's folks? They'd still be there, and we might be too.

We had to go to Duluth. We couldn't cross borders, so we couldn't fly. The only choice left?

We had to drive.

Now, to give you an idea of how remote Key West is, the shortest practical road route from there to Duluth is nearly 450 kilometers, something like four hours' drive. The better route is 500 plus.

Can you say nightmare?

We needed two vehicles, so you had the problem of doing a convoy even if only on a small scale. Then you had the problem of who rode with whom. Cass and I were going to ride together; that was as certain as the sun rising. This meant we had to ride with her parents, because my parents had a three-seater they'd bought when it became clear I wasn't going to be leaving them any time soon. Their other two vehicles were little two-seaters.

That left the problem of Shawn, because him plus Cass plus me for four hours would result in bloodshed, probably his. He didn't want to ride with my parents; fair enough, I suppose.

The wrangling continued for a couple days, which I was vaguely aware of. In the end, Dad went over to Grand Forks with Mama. They rented a vehicle big enough for everyone to ride in and keep us separated: an RV.

Yes, we still had RVs when I was growing up. In fact, we *still* have them. They just won't die off, because there's always a percentage of the population who wants to get up and go places without being tied to hotels and the like. They're a bit more advanced than the boxes on wheels from the 20th and early 21st centuries, and much more efficient too.

Gotta put on my adult hat here. After the Green Wars, hydrocarbons as a fuel source was pretty much dead. The EV revolution of the Thirties had dropped the percentage way down, to about 25% of all vehicles, but there were still some segments of the market which were dominated by gasoline power right into the '70s. RVs were one of these, but even they had to adapt.

The manufacturers were clever, I'll give them that much. When faced with the inevitable, they adapted. Electric motors on every axle gave enough power so the cliché of "too big to get out of their own way" no longer applied. Batteries were built into every flat surface: under the body, in the walls, in the ceiling, provided buckets of power. Solar panels on the top let it recharge en route, and a hydrogen fuel cell linked to a generator meant you never ran dry. Plus you could plug in overnight to boost the charging speed.

The model my Dad got was big. No surprise, right? Seven people, and three of us had to be kept separated, which is why he couldn't just get a van.

Cass and I took the bedroom in the back for ourselves. We spent all four hours playing, mixed with some reading and watching the world go by. Occasionally we could hear Shawn whining about being stuck with adults and giggled about it. Maybe it wasn't terribly nice, but he couldn't hear us through the door.

We loaded into the RV right after breakfast and were in Duluth at lunchtime, so we ate and then went to the NIDoS (Northern Imperium Department of State) building for the photos and processing.

I don't actually remember too much about the afternoon, just that it was long and boring. We had rooms in a hotel overnight, and we promptly claimed a room of our own. While we were wating to check in, Cass said, very loudly and with no self-consciousness whatsoever, "I'm not sleeping with my brother!"

So we got our own room.

I think Shawn won, though, because *he* got his own room, too.

The next morning we all trooped over to NIDoS and waited.

And waited.

And waited.

And that's when the problems could have *really* started, because if there's anything worse than a couple of bored six-year-old girls, it's a couple *smart* and *curious* bored six-year-old girls.

We wandered off. Maybe we didn't entirely wander. We said we were going for a walk. Distracted by Mama, Dad sort of waved at us. The adults were all busy talking adult things (boring!) and not paying attention.

As we walked, we learned something new. Back home, everyone knew us and had known us all our lives. They knew exactly what we were capable of and took that into account. But with these new people? We were smallish and cute. Anyone we saw who might have turned us back just smiled at us and let us go.

I mean, what trouble could we be?

Well, we toured the building for a while, poking our heads into any room we could open and saying hello to anyone we saw. We rode an elevator for I don't know how long, maybe a half hour, entranced by the novelty. How did that distract us for so long? It was a tall building, the tallest we'd ever seen, and some of the elevators were on the outside. We could see everything once we'd gotten up a few floors. Admittedly, it wasn't much more than the docks and the beginnings of Lake Superior, but we were six. It was cool to us.

Eventually we bored of the view and exited on the top floor, which was the dining commons for their high officials. We'd already found the cafeterias for the regular bureaucrats on lower floors, which we thoroughly explored.

This place was *nice*. I mean, white tablecloths and linen napkins nice. Silver silverware nice. Crystal water glasses nice. *Far* too nice for us, and we knew it, so we were about to leave when a voice called out to us.

"Young ladies!"

I wanted to ignore it but Cass was too polite. She turned and said, "Yes?"

"Come over here, please." It was the only person in the room, other than a server standing against a wall trying not to look too bored.

We went. This was an adult, after all, and not only an adult but one with the air of someone who was used to being listened to. Besides, he was sitting down and in a good suit; worse came to worse, we could outrun him.

"What are you doing here?" he asked.

"Just looking around," I answered. I figured the truth would be good, but not all of it. He might not appreciate knowing we'd been wandering the halls of the building.

"Visiting?"

"Yes, sir." Always call adults Sir or Ma'am, I learned. Makes 'em happy.

"Hungry?"

He said the magic word. We were both in the middle of a growth spurt which would end up putting about a dozen centimeters on each of us. That winter, it seemed I was always hungry, and so was Cass.

"Yes, a little." Never admit to how much you could eat; I'd learned that, too.

"Well, sit down and keep me company."

We did.

Oh, the food was wonderful! He told us his name was Mr. Davis and he was the Consul, whatever that meant. We sat and chatted and ate whatever he ordered for us. He told us stories about the jobs he'd done, all over the planet, and how this was his last post before a nice, quiet retirement. We told him about our summer of adventures on the trike, and he laughed and laughed.

I think he enjoyed it more than we did. The NIDoS tower was modern and fancy, yes, but it was also pretty sterile, you know? Businesslike?

I think he was lonely.

When we were done he said he'd bring us back to our parents. We rode down the elevator together, smiling and happy and still talking, and he guided us to the passport office. Our folks were still waiting, and they looked at us being escorted and suddenly there were storm clouds rolling onto their faces.

"We're not in trouble!" I said immediately.

Cass added, "No, we were with Mr. Davis, weren't we?" and looked up at him with that smile.

"Yes. Charming young ladies," he said, and then he did a double take.

"Hal Briggs? Is that you??"

Turned out he and Dad had served somewhere very hush-hush years ago. Our new friend was thrilled. He stood and talked with them, and talked, and talked! Finally they ran out of words, at least for a bit, because he asked, "Why are you here?"

Dad explained they were waiting for their documents and the visas and Mr. Davis got all red in the face; he knew how long we'd been there, since we'd been with him for a chunk.

"I'll clear this up," he announced and he marched over to the window.

The bored attendant didn't even look up, simply said, "Take a number and wait to be called for service."

"How long until the Briggs and Cassidy passports are ready?"

He still didn't look up, nor did he check his terminal for information. "They'll be done when they're done. Sit down or I call Security."

"Your professionalism is sorely lacking," Mr. Davis said, and something in his tone must have set off alarms. The attendant actually looked up.

"Who are you? If you're waiting for a passport, you have to have a number and wait to be called. I haven't called you."

"Please get your supervisor."

That penetrated the hair gel.

"Whatever, they'll tell you the same thing as I just did." But he got up and disappeared.

In a couple minutes he returned with an older woman, presumably his supervisor. He was talking rapidly, probably trying to get his story in before she could hear the other side. She was nodding, but the nodding stopped when she raised her head and saw Mr. Davis.

"Consul Davis," she said, all obsequiousness. "You asked to see me?"

"My friends have been waiting for several hours for their passports and visas," he said, stretching the truth a bit. "And your associate won't give any sort of answer."

"I'm certain they're almost ready," she said, trying to calm the waters.

"Ms. Quen, I know how your department works, and I'm certain they're ready now but sitting in someone's OUT box waiting to be picked up. Get them."

She disappeared, returning in a moment with all the documents.

"Thank you." He took them and handed them to Dad before turning back to the cowering supervisor. "I'd like you to clear some time on your calendar for a meeting tomorrow to discuss customer service. Nine o'clock. My office."

He turned away before she answered, dismissing her, and then he was all charm again. The adults talked for a bit more before Mr. Davis said he had to go back to work and Dad said we had to leave, too, so we might get home before dark.

That was the end of the great passport adventure. We still had a couple weeks before our big trip began, but now it was really real!

Jumping to Orlando

THE BIG DEBATE, AFTER the passport trip, was how to get to Florida. The issue, believe it or not, was the RV.

The original plan, which Cass and I were thrilled about, was to drive to Grand Forks, then ride a jump bug to Orlando.

Maybe I should explain about jump bugs.

The Green War pretty well killed off the airline industry as it existed in the first half of the 21st century. The reason fossil fuels, specifically hydrocarbons, were used for so long is because they're hugely efficient in terms of power potential. A gallon of gasoline, for example, weighs a little under three kilograms but contains 125,000 BTU of energy in the form of heat. For comparison, ethanol contains 76,000 BTU for the same gallon.

After the War many smaller applications of petrochemicals were converted to Hydrogen fuel cells. Hydrogen is more efficient than gasoline in terms of BTU per kilo, but has two major problems of its own. First, Hydrogen doesn't exist naturally on Earth in its pure state; it has to be separated out from other compounds. This takes energy. Second, to transport the Hydrogen it either needs to be hugely compressed or refrigerated to a liquid state.

The aviation industry looked at these problems, added the institutional memory of the Hindenburg, and said, "No thanks!" Then Boeing and Airbus went out and bought up all the companies which had been building the semi-ballistic cargo carriers. Then came the redesigns, but in a couple years most of the airplanes carrying passengers were the jump bugs.

They're not particularly aerodynamic, at least not in the sense of any kind of lifting body. They're intended to punch vertically through the atmosphere, coast through vacuum in zero-*g*, and then blast their way back down to their landing spot. In a way they're a throwback to the science fiction of the mid-20th Century in that they land under power.

Anyways, most airports were converted to jump ports in short order. Only the extreme short-haul routes remained the province of actual airplanes, and no way was Grand Forks to Orlando short haul!

As I was saying, though, we were thrilled by the idea of riding a jump bug. Me, I loved the thought of the speed, and Cass kept saying she was going to look out the windows at the stars.

Once we took the trip to Duluth in the RV, and suddenly Cass's folks were full of arguments why we ought to drive to Florida. It would be fun, they said, it would be a gradual transition, it's almost a vacation by itself. And their clincher, in their mind, was they'd take the RV and leave us in Orlando while they went to Key West.

Dad vetoed it.

We were having dinner together every other day and I think it was Charles who brought up the idea again. He'd even gone so far as to map it all out, and had put it on the table for us kids to *ooh* and *ahh* over. Clever, right? Get us excited and it would be harder for Dad to say no?

Didn't work.

Dad pulled out the one detail which Charles and Tammie had forgotten: their visa only allowed them to go from the Imperium to Big Sky, the closest country which maintained ties with the Confederacy. There was no direct travel permitted between the Imperium and the New Confederacy. The two had maintained a frosty relationship for years, dating back to the Second Civil War, and while citizens of the two countries were permitted to enter the other they couldn't do so directly. Couldn't do it by air, couldn't do it by land, couldn't float down the Great Lakes to the St. Lawrence to the Atlantic and go the long way. You couldn't leave the Imperium and arrive in the Confederacy without an intermediate stop.

The Cassidys had been on the No Travel list the IAB maintained for years and only Dad's influence had permitted them to get permission to leave for the trip. The only country to which he could wangle a visa was Big Sky. Travel from Big Sky wasn't a problem; once they were out of the country they could do what they wanted.

But there was no way they could drive the RV from the Imperium to the Confederacy. Sure, there's a border between Illinois and Kentucky, but they'd never get across. They couldn't get into the United States because their visa didn't permit it. That cut off most of the other land routes.

The only other option would be to drive South through Big Sky, into the Republic of Texas, across the Border States and into the Confederacy. Dad laid out the three problems with that: Texas wouldn't let them in. The Border States were worse then than they are now; it was only a few years after the Nameless War and the gangs were still fighting over control.

And nobody from the Border States was getting into the Confederacy.

So the idea died there. I watched it all with big eyes, but it didn't stop me from eating dinner. And dessert. Couldn't skip dessert.

Planning continued in the background, Cass and I counting down weeks, then days, then hours.

Finally it was The Day.

Cass and I and Shawn helped mostly by staying out of the way. We were each given a single small bag which we could pack with whatever we wanted, but our parents did all the important packing. I guess they didn't want us forgetting to pack underwear or something. Actually, it's more like we would have packed too many heavy clothes, since we'd never known anything but Minnesota weather. Minnesota in winter? The joke is it's so cold in December the cows give ice cream.

At about ten a transport pulled up, a big van, and we all piled in. Cass and I sat all the way in the back where we could talk and giggle without anyone listening. My mom and Cass's mom were in front of us, her dad and Shawn in front of them, and Dad sat up front with the driver. It was a slow drive; Minnesota, winter. Ice. Snow. Bleah. But we got to Grand Forks in an hour.

Getting checked in for the jump was – you know, I was going to say easy, but I really don't know. I didn't do anything except hold Cass's hand and look around. I don't want you to think I was a total hick, but this was unlike anywhere else I'd ever been. Cass, too, and her head was pivoting like an owl's.

There were people, of course, and I'd seen more people than that at the county fair the previous summer. No, it was, well, the sense of *purpose* everyone had. There were queues and desks and kiosks, things going this way and that, and always the announcements!

Grand Forks isn't a big port by any means. It's barely a terminal when you compare it to ones like Houston, or Phoenix. But I was in awe.

After a while, Cass acted like she knew it all, and maybe she did. She probably researched the hell out of it; in fact, I'm sure she did. She was telling everyone who could listen every detail about anything she saw. Once she'd recited all her information, she calmed down a little, but then Dad came back and we went through Customs and she started right back up again.

I've learned over the years that Customs officers are not ones to take a joke. Period. They have their senses of humor surgically removed when they take the job, I think. But we didn't know that, and of course we kids were asked questions.

So when this one officer asked Cass if she'd ever entered Big Sky illegally, she said yes.

That stopped the process dead in its tracks.

They huddled up. After all, who expects a six-year-old to admit to violating a border?

"When did this happen?"

"Last summer," she says.

"What was your purpose for entering Big Sky?"

"I didn't mean to! I was riding; she was driving," and she points to me and now I'm the center of everyone's attention.

"You were driving?"

"Uh-huh."

"You mean riding. You were riding your bike, right?"

"No, I was driving. I'm a good driver," I said.

Again they huddled, and I could see one of them tapping away at a terminal.

"There's no record of your entry into Big Sky," says the one who did the data search, and no wonder. I'll bet the officer who pulled us over simply dumped the record of the stop and never made any kind of official log. I mean, what was he going to say? "Stopped two five-year-olds driving on highway for improper border crossing and possession of an illegal plant?"

I didn't know what to say to this, so instead I pitched my voice higher and said, "I want my Dad. Can I have my Dad, please?"

Which brought him right over and I saw his face fall, wondering what kind of trouble I'd gotten myself into this time. Then he talked to the officers, explaining everything that happened but I couldn't actually hear him. Then he raised his voice.

"There is no record of a border violation? Then what's the hold-up?"

Which was true enough. We were six; we weren't under oath, and our testimony would certainly have been thrown out of a court if it ever went that far. Grumbling, and visibly unhappy, they waved us through.

Dad walked us both out of the checkpoint and well away before he stopped and knelt to look us both in the eyes.

"Girls, don't talk about your little accident with the border. It might cause problems. Okay?"

"Okay, Dad," I say, followed by Cass's, "Okay, Mr. Briggs."

We got to the lounge and she and I rushed to the window overlooking the field. There were all sorts of ships out there, passenger bugs, cargo bugs, some airplanes.

"Which one is ours?" I ask, and Mama showed me the walkway from the lounge out to the bug. With something new to say, Cass started telling the entire lounge about it and how far it can travel and how fast and every other detail she's memorized about them.

Presently, we were loaded into the bug, but there was a glitch. Of course. It seemed that they'd screwed up when they were assigning seats.

I've got to explain about the labels on the seating. They'd done away with the airlines' First, Business, and Economy labels and gone with things more space-y. Economy was now Astronaut; Business was Voyager; and First was Explorer.

Well, we were all supposed to be sitting in Voyager class, because it was more comfortable and had better views out than Astronaut. Somehow my ticket and Cass's had been upgraded to Explorer.

We were *ecstatic!* But there was a problem.

See, Explorer was on the deck right below the crew decks, and Voyager the next level down. The glitch was passengers weren't allowed to move between decks during the flight. The first issue was they couldn't, because of the *g* forces, then during the coasting phase, well, most people were going to be dealing with spacesickness. So we'd be on the top deck and everyone else would be on the deck below.

Dad tried to talk one of us into moving down so an adult could sit with the other one. No go. These were *our* seats, the woman said so, and we were *not* going to not sit together! Then Dad got sneaky and tried to convince the agent to let two of the adults sit there instead of us. But the agent, whose name I still remember, told him he couldn't change the seating assignment now we were in the lounge. So sorry; it could have been done at check-in, but it wasn't and I can't do it now. His name was Steve Miller and I think I fell in love with him just a little bit because of those words.

After a final, "You two behave!" from Dad, we took our seats with huge grins on our faces and stares from the other Explorer passengers.

The window was only maybe twenty centimeters by thirty, not much bigger than a book, but it was big enough for both of us to press our foreheads to peer out. We stayed there, glued to the sight, until the attendant told us we had to sit and strap in. We did so with barely contained eagerness; strapping in meant we were going to be launching soon!

First came the safety lecture. You know the one, don't you? It's a little different for a jump bug than an airplane. "In case of loss of cabin pressure, stay strapped in. Do not attempt to move about the cabin. Automatic systems will deploy to seal the leak, if possible." No oxygen masks; if we lost pressure at 100 kilometers above the surface, we were pretty well dead and a mask wouldn't help.

"In case of an unpowered reentry, remain seated and cover your head with your hands." In other words, tuck your head between your legs and kiss your ass goodbye, because an unpowered reentry means we're either burning up or smashing into the surface; either way, we're done.

We didn't know any of this, so we listened carefully and made sure everything was where it was supposed to be, and then it was time.

The first sign we were really going was a low rumbling, felt more than heard, as the booster rockets ignited. Then the rumble became a growl and the growl became a roar and then we had all the weight in the world pressing down on us and I just about managed to turn my head to see Cass smashed flat into the seat just like me but with the biggest happiest smile on her face.

Boost went on forever and lasted four minutes, then we were on our ballistic arc out of the atmosphere and over to Florida.

I've never been prone to spacesickness. Ever. Zero-*g* simply doesn't bother me. Cass, well, she wasn't happy, but she wasn't sick. She simply didn't want to move overmuch. The rest of the people? Well, they weren't us, so I wasn't paying attention.

When I could I unstrapped my belt and floated over Cass to the window. We'd lucked out and were at just the right angle to see both the Earth below and the horizon and stars beyond.

I'll never forget that view.

There was our beautiful planet, streaking by below, golds and whites and browns and greys changing, as we watched, to greens and browns and blues as we streaked southward. I could see the tops of the clouds, white and fluffy, dark and angular, storms and drifts and curls. Cass was trying to point out details and names but I told her to shush, I just wanted to look, and eventually she did.

Mostly.

I could hear her whispering the names to herself, and that was fine. It made her happy to say them, so why should it bother me?

Far too soon we were being instructed to return to our seats and prepare for re-entry. I buckled in and leaned as far over Cass as I could still manage, watching as the bug pivoted. I lost sight of Earth but was treated to a full view of the stars in all their glory.

I had never known they could shine so bright.

Then the retro-rockets fired and we were kicked back into our seats. Gravity returned with a vengeance, though I suspect it was much to the relief of many, and then it disappeared again. Free-fall only lasted a few seconds this time, then Earth stretched out her fingers and drew us back in. We descended, falling backwards out of the black, the sky gradually turning bluer and bluer. We passed through a cloud, a hazy impression which whipped past in an instant.

Then gravity decided it wanted our attention again and smashed us into our seats, the rockets firing, screaming their defiance at the ground rushing to meet us!

And we were down, not even a bump to mark the transition, only the sudden cessation of noise. Then the attendant was speaking, saying, "Welcome to Orlando McCoy International Jump Port."

"But he just got here?" said Cass.

"Um," was all I could say, completely stumped. I never did figure that one out.

Then it was on to Disney!

We Didn't Do Anything!

I DON'T REMEMBER MUCH about getting from the jump port, the old McCoy airport, to Disney. It was all a blur of sensations and impressions, but one thing I retained? It was *warm*. Like, summer in Minnesota warm! The sun was shining and there was green out there.

In December.

To my six-year-old mind, it wasn't natural.

Cass's parents said goodbye to us there, before we exited the port. They had another jumpbug to catch. I don't think they expected the casual, distracted farewell they got from Cass and Shawn, but there was too much for us to take in to pay proper attention to them.

Dad hired transport; I recall him saying, during the planning, that he was not going to do battle with the idiots who populated Florida's roads. I didn't know what he meant, but looking back with an adult's perspective? Yeah. Smart man, my Dad.

It was a nice roomy transport, too, with just the five of us., and us three kids spent the whole drive with our heads on swivels trying to see everything. Admittedly, this was central Florida; there wasn't much except places to separate tourists from their money and roads to get you there, but it was different.

For one thing, as I said, it was December and we didn't have to wear four layers of clothes. Even stranger, there wasn't snow on the ground!

Frankly, that would almost have been enough. But then we entered the park, and everything changed.

If you're reading this and hoping for a description of the wonders which are Disney, I'm afraid you're going to be disappointed.

Without even touching on the whole corrupting the timeline thing, which Cass (my Cass, my now Cass, not the childhood Cass) assures me is a real concern, there's simply no point. Either you've been there in some reality and know it, or you've never been and won't believe me if I told you. Okay, maybe I'll tell you a little.

Things To Do were not lacking for us.

Dad decided we'd stay at their remodeled Hawaiian Village Resort. This was the successor to their Beach Club Resort, but with some major improvements. It used to be a kinda fancy hotel, back in the first half of the century. What they did when they remodeled was to add some individual villas, outside the main body of the hotel. Basically, they were small houses, but with this sort of South Pacific feel to it.

We loved it.

There were four bedrooms: the biggest and nicest for Dad and Mama, with one each for Cass, Shawn, and me.

Not likely. Separate Cass and me on vacation? Ha.

The big room was on the ground floor, making it convenient and easy for my folks. As I've said, my parents were getting on in years when I dropped into their lives, and so weren't about to go trooping up and down stairs if they didn't need to. As a direct result, we three were upstairs. One bedroom, the fanciest, had an attached bathroom, a luxury none of us dreamed of back home. The other two bedrooms shared a bathroom between them.

Shawn thought he ought to get the big room. He was the oldest, after all.

We had a polite discussion about this.

Then it got less polite.

Then it completely devolved and ended up with me tackling him, pinning his legs to the floor, while Cass sat on his chest. We stayed like that until he agreed to take one of the other bedrooms.

Problem solved.

Oh, don't get all weird on me. We were *six*, fer gossake, best friends who did *everything* together from the time we could toddle. We had sleepovers all the time, I may have mentioned. We always shared a bed or sleeping bag if we were outside, which we were on those lovely summer nights when the weather was just about perfect. Us sharing a king-sized bed on vacation? We didn't think twice.

In retrospect, I think Shawn got the better room. Yes, we had a wonderful view of the lake and the trees, but his room faced EPCOT, and he got the fireworks every night out his window.

On the other hand, we had a balcony.

In the end, we were all happy.

I will say this about Disney itself: they did a fabulous job of making the park safe for kids to run loose. Officially, of course, all children were supposed to be escorted by parents, and the employees kept an eagle eye on the kids swarming the rides. But my folks weren't stupid; I think I've alluded to this. They were also older, and they knew damn well they wouldn't be able to keep up with us if we decided to take off. Their solution was to make rules for us, sit us down the day we arrived, and drilled them into us.

Shawn would stick with them, which caused much grumbling from him. They sweetened it by adding they'd go with him to anything he wanted to do, and miraculously the complaining ended. He knew when he was getting a good deal.

They didn't try to separate Cass and me in the park, knowing it would be futile. Our deal was we were to wear a pair of bracelets at all times: shiny, sparkly things that said Friends Forever. We put them on eagerly enough.

Smart, right?

No. It was genius. Absolute genius. What they didn't tell us, not until years later, was they could track us anywhere within like ten kilometers, so we had freedom without actually being free.

We didn't care. They gave us money each morning, our allowance for trinkets, and they'd done some sort of plan so we got to eat in the park just by showing our passes, so off we went into the wilds!

The first day we tried to ride everything. We encountered Shawn and my parents once, no, twice: once at lunch, and once in passing, but other than that we were on our own and running! Well, when we weren't being watched by the employees.

We got back to the villa around seven and were asleep by half past.

After that, with a little advice from Mama, we took it easier. She told us to look the night before at where we wanted to go the next day. She also pointed out we would be here for ten days, and there really wasn't any hurry to see it all *right now*.

With that advice, we had fun!

The next days were a blur. Rides, food, exhibits, we did it all.

On the seventh day, we didn't rest. We decided we were going to go back to the Star Wars exhibit. It was getting pretty creaky by then, having been up for almost seventy years, and so was pretty much deserted. The first day we visited it, I think we saw a half-dozen other guests. By now it was our third return, and the park workers were used to seeing us. We were familiar, and being young and innocent-looking, we received lots of smiles and waves. If we wanted to they'd let us ride over and over again, at least until someone else showed up.

I loved it, of course. Even at six, I knew what the whole Star Wars universe was and had gone on and on to Cass about it. Kinda like how she'd been on the jump bug.

We're there, and we're doing the *Millennium Falcon* ride for the third or fourth time when Cass suddenly dove into the electronics.

"What are you doing?" I yelp, worried she's going to do something and ruin the ride. "We're coming to the best part!"

"It's not real enough," she said without surfacing.

"It's plenty real!"

"I can make it better. I've figured it out."

I should have known I was in trouble at that point. Instead, I said, "Okay," and returned my attention to the show. It was really neat; it shook you around, like you were really flying, and was my favorite part. We went through three full cycles, about twenty-five minutes, and finally Cass emerged from the panel she'd opened.

"What did you do?" I ask.

"You'll see." The lights went down and the rumbling of the engines began, but this time it's louder, and the seats are really shaking, to the point I'm glad I have my harness on.

"Wh-wh-what d-d-did y-y-you d-d-do?" I manage.

Cass sits in her seat with this evaluating sort of look, like she was checking to see if her tinkering was doing what it should. I guess it was, because she said, "Hang on."

Then it began.

The ride, well, if I don't tell you a little bit about it, you won't believe what Cass did. It was an old-fashioned sort of virtual reality, where a scene is projected on screens mostly in front of you and the compartment you're in is lifted and moved around to simulate the movement on the screens. Like a roller coaster that doesn't actually go anywhere.

All the movements are carefully controlled to not match the visuals and provide just enough of a thrill for the riders without actually doing anything to hurt them.

That's the way it *had* worked. That was before Cass opened it up and connected her padd, let it learn the architecture of the program. From there, it was almost easy for Cass. She took all the safeties offline and convinced the control mechanism not to care. This made the movements to be more extreme. When we were supposed to swoop, we swooped. When we were supposed to bank, we banked. When we were supposed to dive, we dove.

It.

Was.

Amazing.

After the first run-through Cass sat back and looked at me, a worried sort of look on her face. She said, "Did you like it?"

I squealed.

"Can we do it again?" I said.

"It'll start up again in a minute," she answered, relieved. She buckled herself in tight.

The second time was even better although we knew what was coming. I know, sounds like it shouldn't have been, right? Part of the thrill in thrill rides is the anticipation of the unexpected? But even though I knew what was coming, and so did Cass, we both screamed with joy that second run!

When it ended I said, "One more?"

Cass looked dubious but nodded, and then the ride started again. She heard something during the second run which I missed, because she was peering around the compartment even as it started. I wasn't paying much attention, though. I mean, *ride*!

We're in the middle of it all and suddenly there was this terrible grinding noise. The ride lurched to a stop, leaving me hanging nearly sideways in the harness. The screens flickered and went black and we're totally in the dark. I felt the straps digging into me and then there's a groaning sound.

"Kendra, stop moving!"

"I'm not moving!" I yell back.

"Oh," says Cass, and I hear her unbuckling her own straps. "Don't *start* moving. Your seat's breaking loose from the floor."

"What?"

My eyes adjusted and I saw her dangling from her chair. She half-drops, half-slides across to the wall of the compartment to my right, catches herself, and pulls her way up until she's across from me.

"Do what I tell you," she said, and I nodded because now I can feel the seat groaning and aching and warping beneath me.

"I'm going to brace the chair with my feet," she says. "When I do, I want you to unbuckle and jump towards me as fast as you can."

"Towards you?"

"Don't argue with me!"

"I'm not!" I'm pouting, even though I know it's silly. All I did was ask a question, after all.

"Ready?" she says.

I move my hands so they're over the releases and feel the seat shifting more.

"Ready," and my voice quavers just a little.

I hear her grunt with effort; she's about 120 centimeters tall, but the base of the chair is about 2/3 of that away from the wall. This was a big stretch for Cass to reach. Once she's in place, I feel the seat wobble less and I know her feet are planted as firmly as she can manage.

"Now!"

I unclasp the belt and push away. I sort of arc forward and down, into the front corner of the compartment. The chair warps backward from my push and I hear a crash, then a sliding sound, but I'm too busy dealing with my situation to look. I get turned around so my back's against the wall but now I'm sliding backwards, head-first down the wall, and trying to grab something, anything to slow me down but there's nothing, just flat slick steel, and then I *whoomf* into Aiyana, all the way in the bottom corner. She'd released her hold on the chair to slide down first, figuring I wouldn't be able to stop myself, and caught me before my head could smash into anything. We both go down in a heap.

We're in a messy pile when the door in the back is yanked open and light fills the compartment.

"Hello? Anyone in here?" says the attendant, pulling himself up and in.

"Over here," Cass says. She might have caught me but she wasn't too much taller or larger than me; she couldn't lift me off.

He looks over and reaches my way. I grab his hand and pretty much monkey my way up his arm to the door. Another attendant is waiting outside and I drop into her arms.

A few seconds later Cass follows.

"What happened in there?" says the second attendant, and I'm about to answer when Cass interrupts.

"I don't know; we were having fun, then the ride got really, well, exciting, and then it stopped."

She looks at me. I pick up on the thread and say, "Yeah, it was cool! Is that a new part of the ride? I really liked it! Until we got stuck. That wasn't much fun." I add a pout.

"Where are your parents?"

"Oh, my parents are in Key West," says Cass, and the girl's eyes widen in horror.

"Do they know you're here?"

"We're here with my parents," I jump in, and I think I averted an all-out crisis. They held onto us until Dad came to claim us; I think they wanted to make sure we weren't hurt. I found out later they gave Dad five lifetime passes, probably to keep him from suing the park. I always wondered why we went there so often for the next several years.

I don't think they ever figured out it was Cass who rewired it, or whatever it was she did exactly. I'm sure they figured out what was done, but there's no way they believed a couple of little girls could have broken their machine. Utterly inconceivable.

Oops.

Just One More Ride, Please!

WE DID *not* want to leave Disney.

Nope.

Even after the near-disaster in the *Falcon,* there was so much to do we didn't get bored.

Which, of course, made it more difficult for my parents to pry us away.

Cass was the least reluctant to leave of the three kids Yes, she was having fun, enjoying more independence than a six-year-old probably should have had, but she also wanted to visit Key West. For my parents and her brother, she maintained it was because it was a beautiful place. Privately, she admitted she missed her folks.

She wasn't pushing to leave, but she wasn't pushing to stay, either.

I was terribly torn.

On the one hand, Cass made Key West sound like paradise on Earth, so I picked up some of her excitement. Her unhappiness about being apart from her parents also gnawed at me, because I was happier when she was happy. On the other hand, *Disney*. Rides. Freedom. Fun. Cass. On the gripping hand, Cass was going to be in Key West, too, so my decision was a bit easier.

Shawn hated the idea and didn't want to leave.

He threw a tantrum which, I swear to Zeus, lasted three hours the day before we were supposed to head out.

It started as soon as we arrived at the park, just before we were going to separate and go our ways, and I haven't the slightest clue what set it off; it might have been Dad saying something like, "What do you want to do on your last day here?"

Cass, the soft-hearted soul she has always been, wanted to stay with him. Shawn was her brother, after all, even though he was always a brat to her.

(Can you be a brat if you're older? Does that work? Or is it only the younger sibling who can be a brat? I don't know.)

Where was I?

Right. Shawn being a brat to Cass. No, wait, that's another story. Shawn having a meltdown is what we're talking about.

Anyway, while Dad was trying to deal with Shawn, Mama pulled us to the side. She gave us that day's money, told us to have fun, not to worry, and we'd meet for lunch.

I was ready to take off; Cass took a little persuading, but only a very little, and we were off. The morning passed far too quickly for our tastes and we ended up reuniting with my parents for lunch right on time.

Shawn was about tantrummed out but not quite. He'd been reduced to occasional bursts of, "I don't wanna!" while my father essentially ignored him, soaking in the Florida weather. When the rest of us sat at the table, he joined and ordered his lunch.

And so his rebellion ended in a whimper.

Toward the end of the meal, Mama pulled me aside and asked if we were going to get any souvenirs; I told her maybe, but we didn't know what. There was only so much we could get with the Dixies she gave us.

"You haven't looked at your money today?" she asked with a twinkle.

"No," I said, confused. I knew better than to count money in front of people, even at six, so I'd taken the envelope and stuffed it in a pocket. It was nice they gave it to us, but we hadn't used much of it since food and snacks and stuff were included with our passes.

"Why don't you look now?"

I shrugged, not understanding but unwilling to argue with Mama. For the visit, they gave us each twenty-five Dixies per day to spend on whatever we wanted. We didn't spend much of it, but we didn't have to give it back, either, at the end of the day. I didn't know what to do with it, kinda figuring I'd get something cool at the end of the trip. I think Cass was planning to save it for Key West.

I pulled out the new money now and counted it. Then I counted it again. Then I looked at Mama.

"Is this right?"

"I don't know, Kendra. What did you count?"

"I counted four hundred Dixies!"

"It's right. Now, half of that is for Cass, so make sure you give it to her."

"I will, Mama, but why?"

"Because it's hers, Kendra."

"No, Mama, I mean why so much?"

"Because we want you to get something special to remember this trip. I'm sure there's something you've wanted, isn't there?"

There was. It was totally silly, but I didn't care. I kept dragging Cass back to the one shop that had it and staring at it through the case.

I nodded to her.

"Then get it today. Do you have enough? Do you need more?"

I thought hard. With the leftover money I saved, I had enough for what I wanted to do, but if I asked for more I'm sure Mama would give it to me. Still. I had enough.

"No, Mama. Thank you." I reached up and hugged her. "You're the very best Mama ever."

She hugged me back, briefly, then let go.

"Go have fun. Be back here at six."

"Why?"

"Special surprise. Don't be late!"

This was unusual; while we'd always meet for dinner, she wasn't usually so specific.

"We won't be!" I promised.

On the way out of the restaurant, I told Cass what Mama told me and gave her her money. She promptly tucked it in her pocket, adding it to the few Dixies she'd brought out with her today. The remainder was safely stashed away in our room.

So we had fun.

Lots of fun. It was the last day, so we hit all our favorites one more time.

At about five, as we were about to queue up for another ride, Cass pulled me aside. "Kendra, if you want to go to your favorite store, we need to skip the ride. Or we'll be late."

I looked at the line; it was short, so short that even standing out of the queue we were almost to the front. I wanted one more ride, but I knew Cass was right, so I sighed and nodded. In a few minutes, we arrived at the store. I went right to the spot where the jewelry was. Cass went off to look at something else; she knew where she'd find me.

There they were.

A matched pair, at least to my eyes.

Two bracelets with one bangle on each.

One was Pepper Potts in her Iron Woman suit, ready to kick ass, but with the helmet down so her red hair was flowing down her back.

One was Carol Danvers, Captain Marvel.

I got the clerk's attention.

"Yes, miss?" he said.

"I want those," I told him, pointing.

"These?" he confirmed, tapping each.

"Uh-huh."

"They're pretty expensive, you know."

"I know. One hundred twenty-five Dixies each." I was proud of myself for noticing the detail.

"Plus tax."

Right. A detail I'd forgotten.

"Uh-huh. Oh, and that one, too." I pointed to another bracelet.

He frowned. This wasn't quite going how he expected it to.

"I don't mean to be rude, miss, but do you have enough money?"

"Uh-huh." I pulled out the money I had and showed it to him, the hundred-Dixie note out. His eyebrows raised, but he didn't say anything more and started pulling bracelets out.

When he had them all gathered, he said, "Do you want these gift-wrapped?"

"Uh-uh," I answered. "Not those two. They're for me and my best friend."

"Let me guess," he said, wrapping them up and putting them in a bag. "She has red hair."

"How did you know?"

"Because your hair isn't."

I pondered his response as he wrapped the last bracelet, rang them up, and made change for me.

"Oh, I get it!" I finally said. "No. I mean yes, she has red hair, but I'm going to give her the Captain Marvel."

"Oh?"

"Uh-huh. When she looks at her wrist she can think of me, and when I look at my wrist I'll think of her."

"Very cute," he said, smiling. "Here you go."

I took the bag and returned his smile. "Thank you."

I found Cass; she was paying for her chosen item, a three-volume set called Imagination's Playground: The History of the Walt Disney Company which probably weighed four kilos.

"What did you get?" she asked.

"It's a surprise." I wouldn't say anything else.

"Stinker."

We left, me carrying two of her books, and were in plenty of time for dinner.

Dinner was nice. It maybe wasn't what three kids would have chosen for the last meal on holiday, but yeah. It was nice. I went back years later, with a girl I was dating at the time, and came away with a much greater appreciation for the food.

I gave Mama the other bracelet I'd picked up. It was cute, silver, with Mom in the middle, because I couldn't find one that said Mama.

I just realized that I ought to explain her name, or what I called her. You know, the whole Mama thing. It seems a little childish, but until I was probably ten or eleven, I always called her Mama. That's just how it was, you know? Then I started calling her Mom like all the other tweens, and then a couple of years later I tried out Jane. As you might guess, that didn't go well and I went back to Mom. Through it all, well, except for the Jane experiment, she smiled and responded however I addressed her.

Many years later, when Cass and I had our daughters it made life easy. Cass was, and still is, Mom, and I'm Mama.

Anyhow. Her bracelet said Mom, and it had the cutest mouse ears. She ooh'ed and aah'ed over it and said how thoughtful a daughter I was.

Dinner ended on a happy note.

Then we went and watched the fireworks display.

Wow.

They did them right.

We'd seen them a couple of times before, but not this close. We were right under them, it felt like. The restaurant had outdoor seating, and we were still at our table – did I mention dinner took nearly three hours? Yeah. Seven courses and all fancy.

But the fireworks were amazing and perfectly synchronized with the music. Disney was old-fashioned and still used chemical rockets for some of their displays, though most of them were drones with lights.

This was the old-fashioned kind.

We loved it.

The whiff of the gunpowder in the air, the *crack* of the explosion lagging a shake behind the display, and the pulse in the air all combined to make it about a perfect ending.

We got back to the villa and got ready for bed. Wearing a giant smile, I told Cass, "Ready for your surprise?"

"My surprise?" she said.

"Duh, silly. What, you thought all I did was get something for Mama?"

I was rummaging through the bag; I had to pull out the right one. Luckily he'd wrapped them in different colored tissue paper and I remembered which was which.

"Here," I said and handed it to her.

She unwrapped the paper. I tell you, even then she was an unnatural person. I mean, it was just wrapping paper which was gonna get thrown away!

And then she saw it.

She held it up so it twinkled in the light.

"It's beautiful," she said. "Who is it? Is it you?"

"No, it's Captain Marvel."

"Who?"

Oh, that girl.

"Remember the movies we saw?" I tried to explain and eventually, I succeeded.

"Oh, her!"

"Uh-huh. Anyways, yeah, she kinda looks like me but, you know. Taller."

"And she can fly."

"And she can fly," I agreed.

"And do the laser eyeball thing."

"That too."

"And…"

"And I got it for you so I'll always sorta be with you," I interrupted before she could list any other differences. Impatient, I finished tearing the paper off mine. "And I'll always have you."

"Oh, Pepper!" she said. I boggled. How could she remember Pepper and not Captain Marvel?

"See? Red hair like you."

"But I don't wear armor. Bet I could build some, though."

I put the bracelet on and closed the clasp. "Never gonna take it off."

She mirrored my action. "Me neither."

Then we moved on to important things: how we were going to torture Shawn on the way to Key West. Dad said we were driving, so there'd be plenty of time.

Joyous.

"Isn't Key West South?"

THE NEXT MORNING, WE left for Key West.

Dad had rented a transport and we all piled into it for the drive.

Yes, drive. We could have jumped, like the Cassidys, but I think Dad wanted us to have some more time to adjust from Disney to not-Disney. Orlando to Key West was, is, a fair distance, over 600 kilometers, and takes the best part of a full day. The worst part is driving through Old Miami. But I'm getting ahead of myself.

We left after breakfast. I don't know if it was their plan, but we all had our favorite foods. Aiyana and I both had waffles, but hers were smothered in strawberries and topped with whipped cream. I'm a purist and had mine with butter and real maple syrup. Minnesota might not be known for its syrup, but there were enough small producers around where we lived that I never had the fake stuff until the first time I was offered it at school.

Ewww.

And bacon. Had to have my bacon. Breakfast without bacon was just fuel. Aiyana had eggs. Shawn decided to be different and have toast and sausage and, of all things, a fried tomato. No idea how he got the idea for a fried tomato; I think he was trying to be mature. He barely touched it.

My point is we got to have what we wanted, as much as we wanted. We were full and happy when we got shepherded out to the parking lot.

Dad was smart, again, and got the same size transport as we'd ridden from the jump port, except this time all the kids got seats to ourselves. At least as to ourselves as we wanted.

Shawn got the middle seat, and boy did he lord it over us, stretching out and saying things like, "Boy, it's nice not being crowded."

Brat.

We didn't care. Mama sat up front with Dad to keep him company, and probably enjoy the relative peace. That left the back seat to us, again, and we were in heaven, once we got out of the city.

Of course, I sometimes wonder what would have happened if Dad hadn't pulled his surprise that day.

See, the easiest way to go is dead south on Florida 91, then pick up Confederacy 95 near Port St. Lucie. Instead, Dad drove East, towards the Atlantic coast.

I didn't know any of this; I was too busy watching everything go by, giggling with Cass, and trying to stay awake. Full bellies after a late night and early morning make for a sleepy Kendra and Aiyana.

But then I saw The Sign.

Big sign.

Huge. Impossible to miss.

Kennedy Space Center 25km

I knew about KSC. It was one of the pieces of real estate the United States managed to hold onto when the Confederacy broke away for good in 2061. Why hadn't they abandoned it? They had developed the next generation shuttles, the ones which lifted using the ground-based laser systems to boost them through the lower atmosphere. All of the launch mechanisms were at Kennedy, and they weren't about to give them up.

What can I say? I was a space junkie, and Cass even more so.

I loved the adventure. She loved the technology.

Between us, there was no way we weren't going to KSC! After a whispered conversation, I unbuckled and went up front. My Dad was driving, so it was my job to ask.

"Dad, can we go to Kennedy?"

"Kennedy?" he said. "Why do we want to go there?"

"The shuttles, Dad!"

"Ohhhh," he said, drawing it out to about four syllables. "Gee, punkin, I don't know. It's a long way away."

"Is not! That sign said 25 kilometers! That means we could be there in, um. Don't tell me."

Division was new to me that year. I could have asked Cass and gotten an answer in a flash, but it was my question, and I was by-God stubborn about things when I wanted to be. "Twelve minutes!" I finally said.

"Very good. You're right, we're only twelve minutes away. Less, now. But are you sure you want to go there?"

"Da-ad!" I managed two syllables, and he laughed.

"We'll go, we'll go!"

I bounced to the back and shortly Cass and I were bouncing together, at least until Mama told us to sit down *or else*. When Mama said *or else* she meant it, so we sat and looked for signs.

Cass spotted the gantry first, one of the old ones, and I raced over to her side to press my nose against the window.

We had to go through Customs, but it was pretty perfunctory. The Cold War between the Confederacy and the US was in a period of quiescence just then and tourism was trying to take advantage of it.

We parked and got out, but not before Dad set down the ground rules. No running off. No separating. No touching things we weren't supposed to touch and don't give me that look, Kendra. No teasing your sister (to Shawn). No teasing Shawn (to us both). We solemnly agreed to everything. We would have agreed to anything, we just wanted to get *in*!

I can still remember every detail, down to the crunch of the seashells lining the paths. We walked through the gates and saw the Garden of Rockets. They had added the recently-retired Falcon 21 and a Super Heavy/Starship combination, and I thought I was in heaven.

Cass was, naturally, providing the technical details about every rocket she could see.

We went around and around and around. It was like the first day at Disney all over again.

We'd gotten there at about ten and stayed until they shut down at five. I think, I'm pretty sure, we were the last people out.

"Well," Dad said. "Guess we're not getting to Key West today."

Cass pouted a little; she hadn't seen her parents in almost two weeks, and I knew she was missing them.

"Good thing I have a hotel booked for us just outside Cape Canaveral. And I think there's a launch tonight. No shuttle," he said over our squeals of delight, Key West temporarily forgotten. "It's just a routine satellite launch. Chemical rocket, even. Not a laser thruster."

We didn't care. It was a *rocket* and we were going to see it!

We pestered Dad with questions until he got tired of it and handed us a commpad. "Look it up," he said, and then he concentrated on driving.

The hotel was at the southern end of the launch facility, and thanks to Dad's foresight we had a room on the top floor, facing North. We ate dinner. I'm sure we did. Mama wouldn't let us not eat, but this detail? Gone in the excitement of a launch. At the appropriate time, we took our places to wait.

Cass found the official launch countdown and had it playing, so we knew exactly when the bird was supposed to leave the ground.

I have rarely been so excited about anything for so long. We were watching, listening, and waiting for almost an hour and I swear I was buzzing.

Finally, at 9:03, we heard those magic words: "...three, two, one, zero, we have liftoff, we have liftoff at nine oh three and eighteen seconds."

The light reached us first, a column of white and yellow light as the rocket rose into the sky, a brilliant silver dart on a pillar of fire. It climbed slowly at first, then faster and faster, reaching into the dark sky, carrying a piece of mankind into our species' destiny.

Finally, maybe thirty seconds later, the sound reached us. A thundering roar I could feel against my chest, feel through my feet, deafening me and drowning out the screams and shrieks of joy. The noise went on and on, the glow fading as it crossed across the sky, until finally, they both disappeared.

Cass and I chatted and chattered on the balcony until we fell asleep. I sort of remember Mama carrying me inside and putting me to bed, but maybe not. Maybe it was a dream. Everything seemed to lack reality after the profundity of the launch.

The next morning we left for Key West, for real this time, and now it was a straight shot down Confederacy 95. A few hours later we were getting near Miami and another potential highlight, or at least a scene we didn't want to miss. See, as the climate shifted in the 21st Century, the sea levels rose, and Miami was only about two meters above sea level back then. The rise, combined with the weight of the city sinking into the sodden ground, meant Old Miami was in serious trouble by 2060. Re-routing what was called Interstate 95 was anathema to the federal government, so they came up with a plan.

They would build levees on either side of the road, ten meters tall, and enclose it with a translucent roof using optical aluminum. There would be drains and pumps all along the route to keep the dry in and the sea out, and traffic for the first time in a century could flow through Miami quickly.

Then the war happened.

The project continued, in fits and starts, through the war. Both sides realized the importance of maintaining the roadway, and so neither performed acts of sabotage like what happened in Richmond and Montgomery. But the roof was never built, and the dikes ended up only five meters high, so driving through Old Miami became quite the experience.

It's not fun.

The permacrete is fascinating, from an archaeological point of view. They are poured by layer, not by section, so there are bands of slightly different-colored permacrete the entire height. Having different layers means water has an opportunity to work its way through the join, leaving wet patches surrounded by evaporated salt crystals all along the twenty-kilometer tunnel.

Back then, we thought it looked like a layer cake with dripping icing. Kids.

The pumps don't work the way they ought, so when there's any sort of rain it takes twice as long to clear out. Until it does you're driving through centimeters of water if the roadway isn't closed down.

With the problems with C-95, even the Confederacy had to give in and come up with an alternative. They built Confederacy 895 through the heart of New Miami a few kilometers inland, and the entire purpose of this massive project was lost.

From Miami, it was a relatively straight shot to the end of the road, down what they nostalgically call US 1, across Cross Key to Key Largo and South, South, always South over the water. Oh, sure, big chunks are over the Keys, but even there you have the feeling the water is right next to you, ready to reach up and grab. If the ocean's playful, maybe it will be a little tap; if she's in a foul temper, you could be swept away and out to sea.

Then you leap. The first major span is between Upper and Lower Matecumbe Keys. Compared to others, it's a relatively small one, a bit less than four kilometers, but all you can see to either side is blue and green water, way below you.

It's magic.

At the end of Lower Matecumbe, you do it again, longer, with a couple of barely-there Keys serving as anchors as you jog a couple of times over eight kilometers.

Another jump after Long Key, longer still, passing Duck Key, and landing on Grassy Key. You trundle along for a bit, thinking it's all over, and gee, that wasn't so bad.

Then you reach the end of Marathon Key and you are up and away, a full ten kilometers, the longest jump yet, nothing beneath you but crystalline seas, the mystery which is Key West ahead of you.

I loved it.

Cass told us all about the hurricane of '35, that would be 1935, which destroyed the old railroad bridge and killed hundreds, which took some of the beauty and replaced it with a ghostly, eerie charm.

And then we were in Key West, and it was time to find her parents.

Key West

KEY WEST. WHAT A TRIP, and I don't just mean the visit we made when we were little. It's the people and the personalities and the attitudes.

Did you know they've been an independent nation since 1982?

I mean, wow. Pretty impressive, really. Tiny little nothing at the end of the road, and they've been the Conch Republic since a century before I was born.

Of course, since they're independent, there are hoops to jump through. We went through three border checks in about five kilometers.

I told you we drove down Confederacy 1, right? The old highway over the sea? I thought so.

Along the way you go through the Saddlebunch Keys, and immediately before you leave the land again there's an exit checkpoint. We sped right through it; getting out is easy. Not much of a checkpoint, really.

As you travel past the Shark Keys there's this weird turnaround thing on one, just towards the end of the bridge. We zipped past. I found out later that it's where people who have issues with their United States visas have to wait until things get cleared up.

Once you're past, you're on Big Coppitt Key and you have to stop. I mean, *stop*. The United States, in the Second Civil War, managed to hold onto Key West Naval Air Station, and so you're now entering United States territory. They're not awful abut visas, generally, but it's a major military base. They are a bit stricter than the Confederacy is about letting people out.

That was fun. The tension in my folks ratcheted up, and Dad told us kids to not speak. For once, we listened. Legally, it's not like they could have asked us anything, anyway. We were all littles and anything we said would have been thrown out of any court. The evidence of a minor is inadmissible in court, except in limited circumstances.

Dad's diplomatic passport shut them up pretty quickly.

We drove past the base, and through an exit port on the far side of Boca Chica Key. Over another bridge, a little one, and we were on Stock Island. Dad stopped at the entry port, which was a funny-looking building with a tile roof and a couple of really relaxed-looking guys in shorts and colorful shirts. Eventually one wandered over to the transport and Dad handed him all five passports, which he stamped.

The stamps said, "Conch Republic Entry" and "Stay a While," with the date.

We were in!

"You want to park that thing at your hotel," he said. "Roads here ain't too big."

"How do we get around?" Mama asked.

"You can rent bikes, scooters, or carts. Pretty much anything you want. Or you can walk. It's only maybe eight kilometers to the other end of the Key."

"Oh."

"Where are you stayin'?"

Dad told him.

"Nice place. Go down 1 past the golf course, turn right at the T and stay on 1, turn right again at Dredgers Key Road, and you can't miss it. Then, like I said, park this and enjoy your stay."

Dad thanked him and we drove on.

The rest of Stock Island wasn't anything special, but then we crossed a tiny little bridge and we were in Key West and it was like a different planet. Cass and I could tell right off, and even Shawn seemed to get it. Suddenly the air was sweeter and the birds louder, the sunshine brighter. It just felt happier, you know?

Cass, of course, gave us all a history lesson.

The place Dad got for us was a resort, with private villas again. Lovely. Right on the water. We unloaded, found our rooms, put our bags away, and we were ready.

To sleep, that is. It was a long day driving down the coast, with a short, exciting night before. Even if Cass and I would have gone, Mama and Dad were wiped out.

The next day, though, started awesome.

Our experience the previous summer with our bodged-together trike thing paid off, and Dad rented us a mini cart, kinda like a golf cart but built for people our size. It was electric, and we were shown how to plug in at certain stands and not others. Once we'd passed Dad's inspection, we got to go explore! Well, after Mama made sure we had our trackers on.

It didn't take long to realize one important fact: Key West is tiny.

I thought *our* Key West was small, but there's a huge difference. See, Key West in the Imperium is a tiny village surrounded by fields for miles in every direction. Key West at the far end of the Confederacy is a smallish city on an island surrounded by water.

Big difference.

Drive outside of our town? You end up in another town.

Drive outside of the island? You better know how to swim.

We loved it, mainly because it was so unlike anything we'd ever experienced. Oh, we'd had that week at Disney, and it was sort of a gentle warm-up, but it didn't fully prepare us. We puttered all over the island, exploring every place we thought looked interesting, gawking at the tourists.

Okay, okay, the *other* tourists, happy now?

There were so many, though! Thousands and thousands, all walking around, and you could tell they weren't native because of the way they dressed and moved. The islanders, the Conchs, moved deliberately, precisely but also sort of aimlessly. They really seemed to embody the idea that life's about the journey, not the destination. The tourists moved with a purpose, as if they had to get to everything as soon as they could *or else.*

We made it to the west end of the island, and there were two huge cruise ships.

You have cruise ships, right?

I thought so.

History has never been my strong suit. I could tell you all about <u>The Love Boat</u>, but ask me about real cruise ships and I haven't the first clue. At least I didn't when I was six.

We'd never seen anything like them, not that wasn't anchored to the ground. These things were *monsters.* Four hundred meters long, they went up at least 20 decks, and looked like they might eclipse the sun!

I parked the cart and plugged it in.

"You wanna go look?"

"Duh," said Cass. We jumped out and walked up to one, the *Duchess of Kent*, as close as we could manage and still stay on the dock.

"Wow," was as coherent as I could manage.

Aiyana wasn't much better.

"It's huge!"

We stood there, spellbound, at the edge of the dock, letting our eyes take it all in. We probably would have stayed there longer, but aAbout then one of the crew saw us looking and came over.

"Hi!" she said, brightly. "You really ought to get aboard."

"What?" I said, ever so helpfully. What was she talking about?

"You don't want to be late. Where are your parents?"

"Back there," I said, and pointed to the Island.

She frowned. "And you two wandered away?"

"No, they know where we are." More or less. We told them we'd stay on the Island, and the dock counted as part of the Island, right? That was my defense, in any case.

She brightened. "Well, let's get you aboard. They're adults and can sort themselves out."

"Okay," I said, thrilled. We'd get to see the inside!

"Kendra!" hissed Cass.

"What?" I did my best innocent act, something I had problems with even then.

"We don't belong on there!"

"So?"

"So?! We'll get in trouble!"

"Never stopped us before." She didn't have a good answer to me, and I pressed my point home. "Don't you want to see what it's like aboard?"

"Well..."

She was hooked. I knew it, she knew it. It was just a question of reeling her in.

"Besides, I'll bet we can get off easy. Look," I said, and I pointed to the gangway. "See? They just walk off."

"Okay," she said, convinced. "This is gonna be fun!"

Stowaways!

OKAY, SO I HAVE THE benefit of *mumble-mumble* decades of hindsight. But you know, there's something I haven't figured out yet, even all these years later. I still don't know quite how we managed to get aboard the *Duchess* so easily.

Yes, we had a crewmember escorting us, and she was diligent about herding us onto the ship. The thing is, we've gone on cruises since then when we get back to Earth, even with the kids. It always struck us how strict they are about keeping track of passengers. We got badges and wristbands and there were all sorts of biometrics to get back aboard.

When this happened? None of that. We were littles, and I guess we were exempt from all those things, because we saw adults with tags and, well, I'm getting ahead of the story. Just one more point, then I'll get back to it: I never made the connection until writing this, but I wonder if *we* were the cause of the change in security?

Anyway, enough about that. You're not here to hear my theories; you want stories!

The crewmember, whose nametag said she was called Debra, led us up the gangway, chatting with us about this and that. Once we'd passed through all the checkpoints, just kinda waved through because we were with her, she said, "Do you know where to go from here?"

She was poised to press the call button on the elevator.

"No." Where would she send us? Probably back to a cabin we didn't have, and that would be a problem.

"Oh." Debra's hand dropped, dismay on her face. She clearly wanted to get back to whatever her duties were. "What about waiting in the Kids Fun Zone?"

That sounded better.

"Okay," I agreed and nudged Cass. She was staring at the ship's plan on the wall. When she turned, she turned on her smile.

"Do you think we can have a map of the ship? I'm sure we can find our way with a map." Cass was particularly convincing when she wanted to be, something I both appreciate and struggle with to this day.

"You can read?"

That brought out Cass's best indignant look. "Of course I can!"

Debra disappeared for a moment and returned with a large sheet of paper.

"I circled the Fun Zone." She wanted to be helpful, but I could tell Cass had other ideas.

"Thank you." Cass took the map and gave it a quick look, comparing it to the plaque on the wall. "Where are we now?"

"Down here." Our helpful crewmember circled a spot on the lowest deck.

"Thank you," Cass said again. "Bye!"

Cass pressed the call button. The sudden confidence in Cass's tone worried her, and Debra got second thoughts. Maybe she had a sudden attack of "Maybe this isn't a good idea" about letting two little girls loose on the ship. "Don't you want to wait for your folks?"

"You said they're adults and can take care of themselves," I said, tossing her words back at her. She couldn't argue.

"We'll be fine," Cass added, holding out the map and pointing. "We go up to here, then turn and go down there. Simple." She did the smile thing again as the door opened, and I think that clinched it.

"You girls have fun! I'll watch for your parents."

"Okay," I say, and ducked into the elevator before she could realize we never gave her any names.

Oops.

Cass pressed a button and the doors closed.

"Where are we going?" I figured it wasn't going to be the Fun Zone.

"It's lunchtime. I'm hungry."

Now that she mentioned food, so was I. We'd been having so much fun exploring we'd forgotten to eat anything properly, just some snacks on the way.

"Me too!" Then I had a thought. "Where do we get food?"

"I'm figuring it out. I think –"

The elevator stopped and the doors opened. Two people got on and we stopped talking, but they just smiled and looked at the button.

"Good, we're going to the same deck!" the man said. "Getting a snack, girls? We are."

If we had grown up anywhere else, anywhere besides Nowhere, we would have been freaked out by a stranger talking to us. I know there's a whole culture of not talking to strangers, and I get why it's there. Cities are scary! But Key West? Both of them, from what we experienced? Nothing scary about new people. Everyone was friendly, or at least polite. Having a sunburned, overweight couple talk to us? Harmless.

"Lunch," I said, emphasized by a grumble from my stomach. Everyone laughed as I turned red, and that was that.

We went up a couple decks before the elevator stopped again. The doors opened and the woman said, "Don't eat too much!"

"We won't," Cass promised. We trailed behind them, Cass looking at the map occasionally. It was a bit of a walk, but shortly we heard the unmistakable sounds of people. The sound got louder and louder, and then we were there.

Well.

Let me tell you. This was a day of firsts. Neither of us had ever seen anything like this before.

Mmm. Maybe an exaggeration. We went to school and ate in a cafeteria with all sorts of other kids. If we didn't bring lunch we went through the line and got food from the choices we had.

But this?

Oh.

Wow.

To us, it was like all the food in the world was there.

And the people!

Now, we knew there were lots of people in the world. I know I've said this, but it bears repeating: Cass is really smart and has been for, like, forever, and I'm not stupid. Knowing there were eleven billion people out there was one thing. Having them all in one room? Something totally other.

Maybe not eleven billion. It just seemed like it to my eyes.

I don't know how long we were standing there, but it was long enough to get the attention of another crew member. I remember his name, too: Alex.

Alex smiled and said, "Do you need help?"

I was still staring, but Cass was more alert. "Yes, we want lunch, but our parents are still busy and we're here alone so can you please?" And the smile again. Damn, she could kill with that!

"Of course. What's your name?"

"I'm Aiyana, and she's Kendra."

"Hi. I'm Alex. Let's find a table for you." He started walking and we followed. "Do you want to look out a window? Ocean or Key West?"

"Ocean!" we both chorused and he laughed.

"Lots of tables over there; everyone wants to see the Key." He led us to these giant windows that looked way out over the ocean, the blue, blue ocean and the sun, and ohmigawd how high up *were* we?

I never knew I had a fear of heights until then. Acrophobia. It's weird, too, because in me it kicks in about three or four meters above the ground, but once I'm really high, like a hundred meters? No fear. If I'm in a ship, either air or space? No fear. It's just that middle distance that gets me.

The table he brought us to was probably forty meters above the water, looking down at nothing but a sheer side below us. Let me tell you, it looked like forever!

Alex's voice pulled me back from panicking.

"Let's take turns," he said. "Kendra, will you come first?"

"Okay." I was totally happy to get away from the window. As my stomach reminded me, I was really hungry.

He led me up to the beginning of the counter, picked up silverware, and went down the line with me.

Oh, man, the food!

There were things I'd never seen before, but there were plenty of things I loved, and I had Alex completely load up my plate with enough food to feed half my class.

Okay, maybe I'm exaggerating again, but I was a happy girl.

Aiyana got the same treatment, though she picked out some different things. Then Alex brought back drinks for us while we chatted and chomped.

"If you need anything else, just wave. I'll watch."

"Thank you."

Dammit, she dimpled.

Once he left, we watched the people. Okay, *I* watched, Cass observed. She saw how they got new plates when they wanted more food. Of vital interest, she also saw where dessert was. After we saw the piles and stacks of goodies, we decided to stop on the, you know. Healthy food. We had to save room for the important stuff.

We figured out we could walk over and get dessert.

Anything we wanted.

As *much* as we wanted.

As often as we wanted.

Oh. My.

First plates cleaned, we went over and just stared. You know?

It looked so impressive from our table, but up close it was *magnificent*.

Where do I start? The cakes, I think. So many sorts of cakes. Layer cakes. Cheesecakes. Carrot cake, pound cake, angel food cake. And then the cookies! All the cookies, I think. Chocolate chip, oatmeal, peanut butter, sugar, frosted, chocolate with nuts, oh my.

Ice cream, too. Soft serve, but we couldn't reach the handles. Hard ice cream that you could scoop.

Oh, and fruit. Pfft. Booooooring!

What drew me in was right smack in the middle.

It was a dark chocolate cake, with three layers. Covering it was frosting so dark it was almost black, rich, and creamy, with swirls and decorations on the top in colored white chocolate.

I had to have a piece.

"Do you want some cake?"

I jumped. There was a crew member in the middle of the display. I hadn't even seen her in there, I was so mesmerized by the desserts and goodies.

"Yes, please!" She must have seen, or heard, my eagerness, because she sliced me a piece that had to be ten centimeters thick. It wasn't a slice, it was a slab. She put it on a plae.e As she handed it to me, I put on my best charming face. "Can I have a little ice cream on it?"

It must've worked. She beamed at me and said, "Sure! What kind?"

"Vanilla!"

What can I say? I'm a girl of simple tastes.

She put a scoop right on top, then pushed it towards me. This time, I took it.

I still haven't the slightest idea what Cass got. My eyes were locked on that cake and the glorious chocolativity of it. I just about managed to navigate back to the table and sit down without drooling too badly.

The first bite was heaven.

So was the second bite.

After that, it got better.

All too soon it was gone, and I was licking the spoon. I didn't, quite, lick the plate. I held a quick conference with my taste buds, then got another slice. It was smaller but just as delicious.

Oh. My.

We finally finished eating, and sat looking at the ocean for a while.

Then I realized the ocean was moving.

Oh. Crap.

Now What?

"AIYANA!" I HISSED.

She was hypnotized by the water and the sunlight, so I said her name again, louder. "Aiyana!"

"What?" My use of her proper name got her attention.

"*We're moving!*"

It only took her a second to figure out what I meant, and then she blanched under her new Florida tan.

"We're moving?" she squeaked.

"Uh-huh," I confirmed. I swept the room, looking for our friendly, helpful Alex, but he was nowhere to be seen. I did see other crew, but we hadn't been chatting to them and I didn't want to expose us as the inadvertent stowaways we were. Unfortunately it didn't look like I was going to have a choice in the matter, as Aiyana's face was clouding up. I knew that look; it didn't show up often, but when it did it meant she was about to burst into tears.

Loud, noisy, disruptive, get-everyone's-attention tears, and I knew *that* would be very very bad.

This pulled me back from my incipient cry-fest.

I peered at the faces, trying to find one that seemed friendlier, and finally settled on one woman who was smiling more than the others. A good sign, I figured.

Now I just had to figure out what to ask and do it before Cass started bawling.

Engage her brain. That's what I had to do.

"Aiyana, what should I ask?"

The incipient sniffle stopped.

"What?"

I explained my thinking, that we needed to get an adult involved, and I could see her thoughts turn from being out to sea to this more abstract problem. The clouds receded.

"We could ask where we're going," she finally offered.

"Wouldn't we know?"

"We're kids," she said, reasonably.

I stood and went to ask, more nervous than at any time since our first bus ride to school.

"Excuse me," I say in the most polite voice I possessed.

"Yes, miss?" she said, looking down.

Trying to keep the quaver from my voice, I said, "Where are we going?"

"Excuse me?"

"The ship. We're moving, where are we going?"

"Oh! We're on our way to our next port."

I have to butt in here; sorry. It's been a long, long time since this conversation, and it still annoys me when people answer a question without actually giving me any information. I mean, it's not like I couldn't figure out we were going to our next port! That was the easy answer though, the one she hoped would get rid of me quickly.

Nope.

Rant over. Back to the story.

"Where is that?" I said.

"Puerto Plata."

Again with the non-answer, at least without any other context. I was getting sick of this *real* quick, and I think she saw it on my face because she followed up with, "That's in the Dominican Republic."

I was over it. I didn't know the Dominican Republic from Denmark. The incoherent scream of frustration was on my lips, but Aiyana had come up behind me and answered before I could erupt. "Thank you. How long until we get there?"

"Day after tomorrow. Excuse me," she said and walked away. Fled. Coward.

We went back to the table and dropped into the seats.

"Day after tomorrow?"

Cass nodded.

"This Puerto place has to be a long way away."

Cass nodded again but waggled a hand, having a better sense of geography than me. She never could resist correcting a mistake. "Sort of is, sort of isn't. I think the ship's just slow."

"What are we going to do?" I was barely holding it together, and now that Aiyana was focused again I could feel the sting of tears behind my eyelids.

"Um." She didn't have a quick answer.

"Uh-huh," I said, and now there were hot streaks on my cheeks.

"Don't cry, Kendra," Cass said. "Please? We'll figure something out."

"How?" I sniffled. This was so not what I wanted to have happen.

"Well, I have the map. Maybe we should find somewhere quieter to think?"

We left the table. I followed her lead while keeping her from running into anyone, her head being buried in the map. We went down an elevator and then forward a long, long way and ended up in a quiet little lounge sort of place. There were terminals and Cass promptly plopped down in front of one.

I had my tears under control, even if I wasn't happy. I knew I would be blamed for all of this, but at least we could sit.

Sitting got old, quick.

"What now?" I asked when my patience ran out.

"Shh," she said, not looking up from what she was doing.

I hated being shushed. "No! What do we do, Aiyana?"

"Sit here and I'll show you what I've found." She scootched over on the seat so I had room. "This is a map of the route the ship takes. See here?"

She pointed to a blinking white dot, just separated from the land.

"Uh-huh."

"That's us, and that's Key West."

"Okay." I'd take her word for just about anything.

"This is where the ship has been." She indicated a blinking yellow line which stretched down the Florida coast, back up to the beginning.

"So?"

"This line is where we're going." Now she pointed to the red line, zooming out so it was all visible.

"Oh." The red line went South for a while, did a big loop, and then returned on the far side of some islands.

"How long until we're back here?"

"We don't come back here, at least the ship doesn't. It goes back to Tampa." She tapped the starting point.

This was too much, and I sniffled. "But what about Mama? Dad? Your parents? They're in Key West!"

"I know, Kendra." My weeping infected her now. We sat, holding each other, and cried. This wasn't what I had in mind; I just wanted to explore. Now, we were two little girls who had gotten in way over our heads and didn't know what to do next.

After a while we stopped. Ran dry, more like.

"So what do we do?" I asked, wiping my eyes with the back of my hand.

"We're going to have to tell someone."

I was afraid of this. Telling someone meant authorities and would inevitably lead us into trouble.

Well, no.

I had led us into trouble; this would lead us into *consequences.*

Of course I didn't think of it like this; I just knew all our families, except maybe Shawn, were going to be upset and angry and I really didn't want to face it. From the look on Cass's face as she said it, her thoughts were there, too.

"I guess."

I couldn't imagine what would happen to us, and I said so.

"They'll throw us in the brig," Cass said with assurance.

"The what?"

"Brig. It's like a jail on a ship. For stowaways."

"We're not stowaways!" I argued. "We just wanted to look when Debra brought us aboard, then we found lunch, and then the ship left! We didn't plan to stay!"

She simply shrugged.

"I don't want to go to jail! We didn't do anything wrong!"

She shrugged again.

"Stop it!"

"What?"

"This!" I shrugged at her.

"This?"

"Yes! Stop!"

"Why?"

I bounced from the seat, unable to contain myself. "You're making me nuts!"

"Oh?"

"Augh!" I think I got a little too loud with the last because Cass pivoted her head around looking to see if anyone noticed us. Fortunately it was a quiet part of the ship and a quiet time of day.

"Shhh!"

"Sorry. Okay. We're gonna be in trouble, I guess. But who do we tell?" I'd never had to tell on myself before. Usually someone else (Shawn) did, or I was caught in the act.

"Um. I dunno."

"What?"

"I don't know! I've never been on a ship like this, I don't know where to go or who to talk to! You think I'm so smart and have the answers all the time, but I don't!" She was crying again and yelling at the same time. "I'm the same age as you, Kendra Marissa Smith!"

"You're three weeks older," I said, stubborn to the end.

"Fine, whatever! But I don't know everything!"

"Okay, okay." It was my turn to calm her, so I sat next to her. She scooched away, but I followed until she couldn't go any further. Then she gave in and leaned against me. It felt good, and I enjoyed the moment despite the pile of trouble we were looking at.

After a while I said, "I have an idea."

She lifted her head with a triumphant grin. "I knew it! What?"

"We go to the Captain. That's what people do when they have problems. Or maybe the Admiral. Which do you think this ship will have? A Captain or an Admiral?" She shrugged, but it didn't bother me this time. I was lost in my thoughts. "I think I'd like to be an Admiral someday. And a pirate. And fly a spaceship, no, I want a time machine!"

She was laughing now. "A pirate Admiral with a time machine?"

"Why not?"

She didn't have a reason and instead asked, "How do you know this? About the Captain, I mean."

"Oh, those old shows I watch."

Her face wrinkled. I hadn't yet convinced her of the joys of century-old pop culture.

"Don't make fun of me!"

She raised her hands in surrender. "Now we just have to figure out where the Captain is."

"That's easy."

"Oh?"

"Captains are always on the bridge." My tone was as confident as I could make it.

"And where's the bridge?"

"You have the map. Duh."

Cass unfolded the map and we stared at it.

"It doesn't say where the bridge is," she finally observed.

"I see that!"

"Any more ideas?"

"Well. They're always up front." I tapped the map. "Probably one of these blank areas."

We peered at it as if it would suddenly make sense.

"We're on this floor," I started to say. Cass interrupted me.

"Deck."

"Fine. Deck. We're here. I think." I pointed to what I hoped was the lounge. "If we go out this way, we're going forward."

"Then?"

"Then? We ask. I think it'll be higher up, so they can see better. Can't hit any icebergs if you can see them."

"There aren't any icebergs near Florida!"

"Yeah?"

"Yeah!"

"Well, even if there aren't, we don't want to, um, run into an island or something."

She gave in gracefully.

"Up and forward and ask?"

I nodded.

"Okay." She stood, then took my hand and pulled me up. "Let's go."

Excuse Me, Are You the Captain?

"THERE'S NO WAY IN."

"I see that."

We were standing in front of a blank wall and were totally confused.

We'd followed Cass's map religiously, moving forward and up to the level we thought the bridge was going to occupy. We'd guessed as best as we could, trying to think of what a bridge would look like, but we didn't ask anyone.

Why?

Even though we knew we were going to be in a world of trouble, we didn't feel like accelerating the process. We certainly didn't want to tell somebody like Debra or Alex. While they might be sympathetic to a couple of weeping girls, we knew they wouldn't have any real power.

Now, here we were, where the bridge should be, and there wasn't any way in.

"Maybe they come up from below?" I suggested. "Maybe?"

"We can look."

We went back and took the lift down a deck, retraced our steps forward, and lo and behold we found a door! Big heavy door. We pushed it open and...

Found ourselves outside on a balcony thing.

I've since learned it's called the forecastle, or if you want to be all salty the fo'c'sle. In any case, we were outside and getting blasted by a warm breeze off the ocean.

Which was enough to make us forget what we were trying to do. Hey, like I said, we were going to get in trouble; why look for it when we didn't have to?

We raced across to the low wall separating us from the deck below and pulled ourselves up so we were leaning out. You know the pose. Head and shoulders over the edge, arms wrapped around and down the front, feet dangling, resting on our chests.

It was glorious.

We weren't going fast, I know, but the sunlight reflecting off the blue water, the sound of the wind and waves all combined to make us feel we were in a magical place.

"Dolphin!" Cass yelled and grabbed my arm.

"Where?" She was already pulling me to one side to see better.

"Down!"

I looked past the bow and saw them. It was a school, no, a pod. A bunch of dolphins is a pod, I'm almost sure. Anyways, fins and sleek rounded backs and occasionally a head or a tail, effortlessly pacing the ship and, to my six-year-old eyes, looking like they were having the time of their lives.

It was purely natural for Cass's hand to rest on my arm.

I don't know how long we would have stood there, mesmerized, but eventually, a couple came out the same door. Our privacy was disrupted, the magic dissipated and we went back to the corridor.

"No bridge," I said, face reddened from the wind.

"No," she agreed.

"I don't know where else to try."

As an answer, Cass went back outside. I followed and watched as she leaned against the rail, facing up and back.

"Hold my legs," she said. I didn't know what she was doing, but okay. I held her legs. Once I had her she stretched as far back as she could. The strain was terrible, and I was about to tell her to come back when she abruptly pulled herself in. I barely managed to shift my arms to catch her as we tumbled to the deck.

"Ow!"

"Sorry," she said, standing and offering me a hand up.

"Why did you do that? What did you see?"

"I know where we have to go."

"Good. Where?"

She pointed.

"Up."

"We tried that. It didn't go anywhere!"

"Quiet. I'm thinking."

This was different from being shushed. I was used to Cass needing to concentrate. Admittedly, quiet wasn't something I was particularly good at. If I'm being honest, I'm still not. But standing there, on the deck of a ship some kilometers away from our families and getting farther away by the minute, I managed it.

For a bit.

Just when I thought I would burst from trying to hold my tongue she jumped down from her perch against the rail, heading back inside again.

"Come on."

I was right behind her, following her in and down the corridor and up a deck.

"Cass?"

"Look for a door."

"We did that. It's a dead end." It was; I remembered the plain wall we had found, on both sides, at the end of both corridors.

"No. Before the end."

I was confused. The corridor was lined with doors, most on one side. It must've shown on my face because Cass explained.

"We want a door that says Stay Out or something."

"Shouldn't we stay out, then?" This might be going too far. We were going to be in enough trouble. Why should we look for more?

"It's the only way I can figure they get to the bridge."

"A secret door?"

"Not secret, just for crew only."

"And we'll go in it?"

"Yes."

I shrugged. It's not like we had much of a choice, and I didn't have any better idea.

We walked up the corridor, looking for the doors we shouldn't pay attention to if we were supposed to be there. We chattered about nothing in particular and tried to look like we belonged. Most of the doors had numbers on them, but we found a couple that didn't. They were marked as closets or for room staff, whatever that was, so we went back down, across, and up the other side of the ship.

Pay dirt.

About four meters from the end of the corridor we found Cass's door. Big sign that said, "Authorized Personnel Only" and "Limited Access", a keypad, and a biometric scanner.

No way in hell were we getting through there.

"What now?"

She plopped down with her back against the blank wall. Facing the door. I slid down next to her.

"Now we wait."

"I hate waiting."

Facing the Captain

I DON'T KNOW HOW LONG we waited.

It probably wasn't terribly long, but when you're six and you know you're in trouble even if nobody else knows it yet, a minute seems like an eternity.

It was more than a minute and less than an hour, and it was forever.

We whispered back and forth, though I haven't the slightest recollection of what we said. I think we were simply trying to keep our mouths busy and minds off our upcoming bucket of pain.

Eventually, the door opened. Despite our positioning we almost missed it. It opened so quietly, sliding into the wall, that it wasn't until the white-uniformed crewman was walking away that we processed what we were seeing. Once the penny dropped, I jumped to my feet and dove for the door. I skidded into the gap as it narrowed.

"Ow!" It bumped against me and slid back into its pocket.

Cass hurried after me and now walked through the door, helping me to my feet when she was through. The door closed behind us with a quiet *snick*.

The space we were in was brightly lit, with mysterious banks of monitors and other equipment I couldn't begin to recognize. We heard beeps and conversation farther forward. I raised an eyebrow at Cass. She nodded toward the noise. With only the slightest hesitation, we went.

The entryway/corridor thingy ended in an open door and we could see the bridge. No, that's not right. We couldn't really see the bridge, because of the brilliant sunshine streaming through the windows on the far side. There were lots of people there, all in white uniforms, all busy, too busy to notice us.

It's not like we were hiding, but we also weren't trying to draw attention to ourselves. We knew we were going to be in trouble. That meant we didn't want to accelerate the process. The realization that every moment we didn't talk to someone brought us farther from our families hadn't sunk in.

We were finally noticed by a man with short-cropped hair, and we had to laugh despite everything at his double-take.

"Who are – Captain!"

An older woman pivoted at his call, then followed his outstretched hand to look upon us. Her eyes flashed annoyance for a moment and then cleared when she really saw us. In a soft, gentle, British-accented voice she said, "Are you lost, girls?"

I nodded. It was true, if not the whole truth. I wasn't looking forward to telling anyone we weren't where we should be. The prospect of telling this woman, with her iron-grey hair and a regal bearing? Even less appealing.

"But this is neat!" said Cass. Her enthusiasm for all things high-tech shone through and the Captain smiled at her.

"Thank you, Miss?"

"Cassidy. Aiyana, but my friends call me Cass."

"Miss Cassidy." Her tone made it clear that Cass wasn't going to be included in her list of friends. She turned to me. "And you are?"

"Kendra. Smith."

"And Miss Smith. I am Captain Curtis. Would you like a tour, before we see if we can get you un-lost? We don't usually have visitors." There was a subtle hint in her voice that suggested someone was going to be in trouble for allowing us entry.

"Yes!" Cass exclaimed. I didn't get a chance to say anything.

She addressed the man who saw us first. "Mr. Shreve? Will you do the honors, then guide them where they need to be?"

"Of course, Ma'am."

He gathered us up and proceeded to explain the function of every station in that bridge in exhaustive detail. In fairness to him, it wasn't by choice. If he'd had his way, he probably would have been done and had us out of there in five minutes.

It was simply his misfortune to have been assigned to escort Cass, who even at age six hadn't met a piece of tech she didn't want to get to know better. She asked question after question after question, and if it for a moment appeared he was going to skip a station she never failed to point it out to him, usually with an ingratiating smile. By the time he finally finished, not only were Captain Curtis and Mr. Shreve likely regretting her generous impulse but Cass could probably have operated any station she'd been shown.

She was ecstatic.

I was bored.

The bucket of trouble hadn't upended on our heads yet so I counted it a win. On the other hand, we weren't any closer to getting off the ship and back to our parents.

(You know, I just this minute realized I never knew Shreve's first name. He never offered it, and we never asked.)

As Mr. Shreve was herding us towards the exit, saying, "Let's get you back to your parents," I stopped dead. Back to my parents. Yes!

"Captain Curtis!"

She'd been watching our progress off her bridge and so was only mildly surprised at my outburst. "Yes, Miss Smith?"

"We're not supposed to be here!" I blurted. Like a bandage, right? Best get it done quickly?

"Yes, Miss Smith, but there's been no harm done." She thought I meant the bridge!

"No, we're not supposed to be on this ship!"

This froze her reply for long enough for Cass to speak up.

"Kendra's telling you the truth."

For the next couple minutes, we took turns explaining how we ended up aboard the *Duchess*, carefully omitting the names of the crew who helped us. I played dumb when pressed for names, easy enough to do as a smallish, blonde, six-year-old girl, and Cass played along. Why? We knew there was plenty of trouble to go around, but they didn't know any better and it wasn't nice to get them sucked in.

I'm not sure Captain Curtis entirely believed us. After all, here we were, two little girls, and we'd managed to get aboard her ship without any difficulty whatsoever? We were living in a time of enhanced security in public places, after a pony nuke destroyed Baton Rouge in '78.

Ha.

She was gentle with the questions, but at the end of it we were both crying again, big, messy, snot-running wails. As embarrassing as it was, it probably tipped the scales in favor of at least listening to us.

After getting the names of our parents, Captain Curtis had us escorted away. This officer, a woman whose name I don't remember, kept trying to get us to admit to playing a prank on them. Didn't happen. Since we weren't, she couldn't shake our story.

After another half-hour or so we were escorted back to Captain Curtis. She didn't look happy.

"Well. It seems you told me the truth."

I started to protest. Of *course* we told her the truth! Why would we choose to open ourselves to this much trouble? Cass put a restraining hand on my shoulder and stopped my explosion. Captain Curtis continued.

"I've talked to your parents. They were starting to wonder where you'd gotten to. It seems they're used to your rather independent ways and weren't too worried yet." She cocked an eyebrow at us, skeptical but willing to believe the word of strangers over a comm line. Adults are weird. "They were surprised when I informed them of your current situation."

We nodded. It sounded like my parents, at least.

"What shall we do with you now, do you think?"

I gulped.

Cass suggested, "Turn around and bring us back?"

Captain Curtis laughed at her.

"No, Miss Cassidy; I have a schedule to keep." She pronounced it in the British fashion, with a soft sh sound, which I found amusing. "I cannot bring you back."

I had a thought. "Can you fly us off?"

"I would like to, Miss Smith, but there is no place for a vehicle to land aboard ship."

"Are you going to put us in jail? In the brig, I mean?" Cass said with a trace of a whimper, and I stopped breathing, waiting for the answer.

"No, Miss Cassidy." I started breathing again. "If you had tried to sneak aboard I might consider it, but you young ladies seem to relative innocents in this misadventure. You shall be our guests aboard the *Duchess*, at least until we make port in Puerto Plata in two days' time. We have a cabin which we shall provide for you. Until we arrive, you may enjoy the amenities the *Duchess* and Royal Lines have to offer, even if the manner in which you boarded her was somewhat irregular. Once we arrive in Puerto Plata a determination shall be made as to the resolution of your predicament."

I worked my way through the big words, arriving at an answer I liked. This was better than I hoped, though the resolution talk was worrying. Then I had a thought which shattered the beginning of my good mood.

"Can I talk to my parents?"

On the one hand I really, *really* didn't want to. I knew Dad would be pretty upset with me, and Mama too (but she was always gentler when I did something). On the other hand, I missed them. I was farther away from them than I had ever been in my life, and I wasn't going to see them for at least two days.

"Certainly, Miss Smith, you and Miss Cassidy both. I told them I would ring back once I had informed you of the plan. If you'll step over here?"

She brought us to a terminal in an alcove off the bridge, punched in a code, and then left.

The screen lit and all four of our parents were there, crowded into the view.

It got pretty weepy then and only a little bit shouty. Dad didn't raise his voice in the slightest, but we didn't miss out on it. Cass's Dad filled in. Other than that? All I remember is they would stay on Key West before flying to Puerto Plata the next day. They'd meet the ship when we arrived. Dad looked like he was planning something, but I wasn't about to ask. I figured it probably involved being grounded forever, or at least until January.

We finally disconnected. I felt much better about our situation, and I think Cass did too. At least we knew we'd see our families again, and when.

Only then did it hit me. We had two days on the ship!

The Volcano Awakens

OH.

My.

Gods.

We had the *best* time the next two days despite everything hanging over us!

Part of that was simply the *Duchess* was a fun ship to be aboard. There were activities and parties and games. They were prepared to keep kids like us busy, all day and into the night. We didn't have any clothes or luggage, so the Captain ordered us outfitted suitably from the onboard shops. It was kinda fun, though everything, including our underwear, either had the name of the ship or the line on it somewhere.

Part was we always had a crewmember with us, ensuring we didn't get into anything we shouldn't. Oh, ostensibly they were acting as our guides, but we all knew their real job: making sure we were too busy to wander away and cause more trouble.

And a third part was we knew we were dead girls walking once our parents finally caught up to us.

Fine, maybe not literally, but this was bad.

Really bad.

Bad on toast.

Not only had we disappeared on them, but when they finally knew where we were we weren't even on the same *continent* any longer!

That's pro-level misbehaving right there.

We did our best to put the looming doom out of our minds. We found it surprisingly easy to do, with the people aboard and all the diversions and entertainments the ship had to keep them moving around and spending money.

There were more people aboard than were within 10 kilometers of our homes, and yet we didn't feel crowded at all since the ship was so big. When you're on something which is almost half a kilometer long you have lots of space to play with. Of course, so did everyone else. The trick, which the *Duchess* and her crew accomplished, was to keep us all from feeling packed in.

But the best part, the absolute best part?

Our room.

I've learned since then that what we had isn't considered fancy. But since we were both half-expecting to be somewhere with cots and a bare lightbulb, what we got seemed like paradise.

It was a balcony room. Cabin. Sorry, I forget, it's a cabin, not a room. Whatever.

We had our own bathroom, we each had a bed, and we had a balcony where we could go outside and look at the sea going by.

We didn't mind sharing a room, of course. Plenty of sleepovers had taught us to appreciate the closeness we could get, the giggly fun we could have, when we were in the same space overnight. We'd shared rooms all through the vacation as well.

Somehow this was special.

Maybe it was the sound of the waves.

Maybe it was being able to see the ocean.

I don't know; I've never been able to replicate it, and I've been a cruise devotee ever since.

At the end of the second day, we went back to our cabin. Once we were inside, that night's minder, a woman named Amber who couldn't have been much more than a teenager, said, "We arrive at Puerto Plata tomorrow morning."

"When?" I asked. I was hoping for very late.

"We'll be tied up by 7 a.m."

Darn. Spit. Blast. My mind went to all the consequences that were gonna land on us tomorrow

"Will you be getting us, Amber?" Cass turned on her charm.

"No, I'm not on duty until nine."

"Oh. Do you know who will?"

"I can find out if you want."

"Yes, please."

Amber left, and I turned to Cass.

"What's that about? Who cares who's coming to get us? We're gonna be in so much trouble when Mama and Dad and your parents meet us!"

Cass simply shrugged. "I was curious."

I hooted. "Curious? Why? Our lives end tomorrow, you know!" Maybe I was a little dramatic. "If I'm lucky, Dad's going to ground me until I'm old, like eight!"

"I'm sure it won't be that long. Maybe until we're seven."

"It's still *forever*," I insisted. "Grounded all summer?"

There was a knock at the door, then Amber let herself in.

"Dominic will be here. Is there something special you wanted to do? Not much is available so early."

"We'd like to have breakfast, please," Cass said.

"I'll make sure Dominic knows. Would six be too early?"

I was ready to yell, "YES!" but Cass beat me to it.

"No, but we might still be asleep."

Amber smiled.

"I don't blame you. Goodnight, girls."

The door closed and we were alone again.

"Six in the morning," I groaned and flopped onto my bed.

"We could go later, but I know you're cranky if you don't get breakfast."

I had to agree. I was, and still am, terrible in the morning without something to eat. That winter we were both in a growth spurt, which meant my morning refuelings went from staggering to epic. On the other hand, if we were going to be lectured by our parents, maybe a hunger-induced meltdown would be just the thing to delay it?

Maybe not. It would be just like my folks to make me wait until after they finished before getting some food.

We talked for a while, both avoiding mentioning tomorrow, before cleaning up and settling into our beds. I insisted on having the door to the balcony open to hear the ocean, and that's how I fell asleep.

Six o'clock came far too early. The knock on the door jolted me from a dream. It took me a moment to remember where and who I was. Cass was quicker on the uptake and called out, "Give us a minute!"

There was a muffled reply.

"Come on," she said, disgustingly energetic and bouncing out of her bed. "Time to get breakfast. Do you think they'll have waffles?"

Even then she knew exactly how to distract me. With the mention of waffles, I was out and dressed in what seemed like seconds, my clothes and a few little things stuffed into a bag and ready to bolt out the door. Cass wasn't too far behind me; she'd packed up everything except her clothes the night before.

Planning. She was always good at it.

We went to breakfast, and they had waffles, so I was a happy girl. Big, fluffy, freshly made waffles with any kind of topping I wanted and about the size of my head.

I ate two. Plus bacon.

While we were eating, the ship docked. Announcements for shore excursions rattled around us, other people hustling here and there so they'd be able to get to their chosen activity. We hadn't paid much attention. Waffles, after all.

Sated, we picked up our bags and reluctantly followed Dominic. We knew what awaited us.

He led us down to debarkation and checked in with the crewwoman at the gangway. I didn't quite hear what was said, but I did catch her saying, "Because the Captain said so!"

Dominic sighed and turned back to us, pasting a patently fake smile onto his face.

"Change of plans, girls," he said cheerfully. "Follow me!"

Up we went, up and up and up.

Yeah, fine, we were in an elevator. It was still a long way up since the hatch was on the lowest deck and we ended up on deck 25. This was as high up as we could go. I knew this for a fact, having explored every inch we could get to on the first of our two bonus days. This was mostly a place for people to lie in the sun and walk around the perimeter of the ship. Instead of going aft (see? I remembered) we went forward, through a door marked Crew Only, and down a corridor. When we were as far as we could go he knocked on a door.

"Come!" It was Captain Curtis and I got angry. What now? We'd been good, except for the whole stowing away thing. We'd behaved!

Cass turned worried eyes to me and all I could do was shake my head.

I don't know, I mouthed.

Then we were inside and it was even worse than I could have imagined.

Our parents were all there. Shawn too.

Cry?

Collapse?

I surprised myself; I rushed over to Dad and wrapped my arms around him. Cass was doing the same to her Mom; I guess we both picked the parent we missed most.

We all stood there for a few minutes, hugging and babbling before Captain Curtis got our attention again. Dad pulled himself away and sat down.

That's when I noticed the scene. It was evident they had been there for a while, as the adults all had coffee and even Shawn had a glass of juice. He was glaring at us with a superior glint in his eyes; he knew we were in trouble and was relishing it.

I stuck my tongue out at him.

"Kendra Marissa."

Mama caught me.

"Sorry, Mama."

Dad took over.

"Kendra. Aiyana."

Gulp.

"We've been aboard since the ship docked, talking with Captain Curtis about your situation and what ought to be done with you."

Two gulps.

"Stowing away is a serious crime, one for which there are no statutes of limitation." He saw confusion so explained. "You are in as much trouble as a grown-up."

Two gulps and a frisson.

"The Captain says she believes you, that you never intended to stowaway."

"Uh-uh!" I agreed quickly. "We didn't! We were looking and –"

Dad cut me off.

"Captain Curtis explained. She showed us the video of you two at the dock, and it supports your story. It was an unfortunate error on everyone's part which got you aboard. You bear some responsibility, as do you, Aiyana, but there is more than enough to go around. You also impressed the Captain with your courage in coming to tell her."

Um. Okay. I guess that was brave. I didn't have time to consider what bravery was, as Dad was still talking.

"That, plus the way you've behaved since, has convinced her not to press charges against you."

I felt the tension leave me. This was real grown-up stuff, and I wasn't ready for it!

"Furthermore, she recognized the inconvenience and expense which this escapade has placed on your families and has prevailed upon her company to make us a goodwill offer, which we have chosen to accept."

Huh? Goodwill? I was lost.

"The line has granted us complimentary passage aboard the *Duchess of Kent* for the remainder of the scheduled cruise, as well as certain other concessions which don't concern you girls."

Wait, what?

Dad finally smiled.

"You're not getting off the ship, girls. We're getting on, and we'll all sail back to Tampa."

He saw the incipient cheer and immediately turned serious again.

"Don't think for a moment you're not in trouble, ladies." He locked gazes with us both until we nodded, then he relaxed. "But it will wait until we get home."

He turned to face the Captain. "Is there anything you'd like to add?"

"No, Mr. Briggs, I believe you've summarized our discussions quite handily. Girls, I'd like to officially welcome you to the *Duchess of Kent*, and I hope you enjoy the rest of your vacation."

She smiled, then Dad, then everyone was smiling and laughing and crying all at once. We were still in trouble, yes, but that was Future Kendra and Future Aiyana.

Present Kendra? She was going on a cruise!

Naturally, Dad was true to his word: nothing was said about our unorthodox method of boarding, nor was whatever our punishment was to be ever brought up. Since our families were aboard, we were relieved of our minders and pretty much had free run of the ship.

Except for the excursions.

There were six more ports, and while I could describe all of them even now I won't. Either you can go there yourself any time and I don't want to spoil them for you, or they've changed so much in the intervening years they're unrecognizable.

Each port had excursions, and we were very closely watched by our parents everywhere we went. As in "not out of our sight" watched closely. We still had fun, though, because we could usually persuade them to do what we wanted. Cass especially, since she was the baby of the family. I mean, so was I, technically, but there were twenty-plus years between me and my next sibling, and they were out on their own.

But Cass? She'd bat those eyelashes at them and open her blue eyes wide. The next thing you knew, we'd be doing what she'd suggested. I can't complain; I benefitted from it too. Besides, it still works on me.

So we enjoyed the cruise, but eventually, it ended and we had to go home and face the music.

How Did This Happen?

WE GOT HOME FROM THE suddenly-extended vacation January 10th.

We were grounded until April.

Actually, we were grounded "until all the snow melted," but Cass negotiated the piles where the snowfalls had been gathered out of the bargain. Good thing, too, otherwise the grounding would have gone until June that year; 2087, it was.

Grounding, extra chores, and the trike was taken apart. No more trips into town for us.

On reflection, we got off easy. It didn't feel that way at the time, but with perspective? Wow.

We went back to school, late, and were immediately the center of attention. Our stories and our tans, completely unnatural in a Minnesota winter, guaranteed us an audience wherever and whenever we wished.

"Kendra," Cass said to me one day. This was shortly after Valentine's Day. This year we'd each made a special card for the other. It was tough trying to keep mine secret, since I wanted to give it to her as soon as it was done.

Right. This isn't about Valentine's Day. It was a boring one, anyway. Weekend. Cass, talking.

"Hmm?" We were in my room; I was watching a show and she was reading. Pretty normal stuff for us. Oh, and it was snowing, which was normal for Minnesota.

"I'm worried."

This got my attention. Cass, worried?

"What about?"

"Mom's been sick."

My attention wavered. Being sick in Minnesota during the winter wasn't a surprise, and I said as much.

"It's a weird kind of sick. She's not sneezing or coughing or any of that normal stuff."

"Then how do you know she's sick?"

"Well." Cass paused. She was usually shy about describing bodily functions and this was no exception.

"What?"

"She throws up an awful lot, usually right after breakfast. Or during. Says she can't keep anything down." She frowned. "But she eats dinner and everything's fine."

I shrugged. "No clue."

I wasn't being crass or uncaring. I honestly didn't have any idea. I knew I needed to cover my mouth when I coughed and wash my hands often, especially in the winter, and we always wore masks at school. But different kinds of sickness? Nope. Not me.

"Why don't you look it up?" I suggested, then returned to my video.

"I will!"

I had no doubt.

That was the end of it as far as I was concerned. Cass didn't mention it again and so it slipped from my mind.

About a month later everyone had gathered at our home for dinner. We did this about once a week, trading locations back and forth. Supper was almost over and we'd just been served dessert, a chocolate crème pie, when Charles stood up. Tammie tried to get him to sit, but he wouldn't.

"Friends, Tammie and I have an announcement."

"Not yet!' she hissed at him. He ignored her. I ate my dessert. Adult things.

"Aiyana, you and Shawn are going to have something in common." The siblings looked at each other in disbelief. They didn't hate each other, strictly speaking, but they certainly avoided each other's company whenever possible. Tonight, for example, Cass was sitting next to me while Shawn was at the far end of the table with my parents between him and me. Other than breathing, what did they have in common?

"You're both going to be older siblings!"

Cass and Shawn shared another look, and then Cass spoke. "Dad, that doesn't make any sense. You can't make me older than Shawn. Even if you could, he wouldn't be the older sibling."

Dad and Mama were grinning. As I thought, this was some sort of mysterious adult thing which we kids didn't have a clue about. There seemed to be a bunch of them, usually surrounding an idea we kids had and providing them an excuse for why we couldn't do it. I couldn't imagine what they might be taking away now. We were grounded and had tried to be good!

The food fight at school was totally not our fault! The principal even said so.

"No, munchkin," Charles said. "Mom's having a baby."

This was a shock.

I mean, a baby?

What did they need with a baby?

And they weren't even my parents!

Cass looked stunned. I took her hand and she squeezed, hard.

"I don't want another little sister!" announced Shawn.

"It might be a boy," Tammie said. "We don't know. We found out for certain a few days ago."

"A brother?" Shawn's tone changed in a flash.

"Maybe," Tammie confirmed. "We'll find out next month."

"It better be a brother. I don't want another sister. One's too many." He glared at Cass. I matched him watt-for-watt.

"A baby?" Cass finally said.

"Yes, munchkin."

"When? How?"

Tammie and Charles didn't even blink in avoiding the second question.

"Late September," Tammie answered. "You'll have lots of time to help us get ready, and we *are* going to need your help. You and Shawn."

"May I be excused?" Cass said, pushing her plate away.

She was shaken. As I said, the dessert was chocolate crème pie, probably Cass's all-time favorite dessert, and she *never* turned it down. Ever.

Forget shaken; she was traumatized.

I followed her to my room and watched as she sank bonelessly to the floor. I managed to catch her before she hit the ground and somehow transformed the catch into a seat, almost gracefully.

"Isn't this good news?" I asked her, genuinely confused.

"I don't know," she said, tears dripping from her eyes. "I don't know how to feel, whether to be happy or sad or excited or scared. I don't know what to do with a baby or what they need or anything!"

I didn't have a good answer, so I held her. Eventually, an idea came to me.

"Well, you have time to learn. Your mom said the baby won't be here for months, not until the next school year, right?"

"Uh-huh." Sniffle.

"Well? Aiyana, you're the smartest person I know. If you can't find out all there is to know about babies and being a big sister, nobody can." I didn't have anything else so I stopped and hoped it was enough.

"Maybe," she agreed. Sniffle.

I was out of my depth and knew it. We sat there for some time. How long? I don't really know. It was long enough for my leg to go numb where I was sitting on it before she was ready to move. I felt her stir and loosened my hold.

"Thank you," she said, stretching and standing. She reached down to pull me up.

"What are you going to do?" I took her hand. "Ow!"

"Did I hurt you?"

I was hopping around. "No, my leg's asleep and it's waking up and it doesn't want to!"

She thought this was the funniest thing and started laughing and laughing. I disagreed, being the one with a leg that felt like it was on fire, but her laughter was enough to prevent me from snarling at her. Pretty soon I started giggling, which increased her laughter, and we ended up on the floor, rolling around until our sides hurt.

I regained my breath at last.

"You didn't answer."

"Answer what?"

"My question."

"What question?"

For a genius, she was being awfully dumb.

"What are you going to do?"

"Oh," she said, finally getting it. "What you said. Look it up and figure out how to be a big sister." Her face lit, a joyous sight even then. "I thought of something."

"Of course you did."

"You wanna be an aunt? Aunt Kendra. You can help me!"

"Do what? And I don't think that's how aunts work." I was an aunt to my folks' grandkids although some were older than me.

"Sure it is!"

I shrugged. When Cass got confident like this there was no point arguing with her.

"Okay. Come on, I want my pie."

I got another piece of pie, too.

Free At Last!

I THOUGHT OUR GROUNDING would never end. It probably would have been shorter if we hadn't been ourselves.

See, Dad played fair. He said we were grounded until April. This meant we were grounded until April 1. All good, right? Right. Then, in late January, I kinda blew out the circuitry in the living room when I drew too much power. Again. I didn't mean to, and it wasn't my fault we lived in a farmhouse that had been built back in the early 20th century with wiring nearly that old. How would I be expected to know that drawing thirty amps would blow it out? But no, I should have remembered the other time.

Hmph.

That added a week to mine.

When Cass poured syrup on Shawn's head in February? Another week for her.

There were a bunch of other add-on sins, a day here, a day there, which all stacked up another couple of weeks for each of us.

It was mid-April, and we thought we'd see freedom. It was so close, we were counting down the days. And then? Shawn screwed up. He picked on Cass.

Again.

That wasn't the mistake. No, his mistake was his timing. He did it in front of me.

I knocked him down and rolled him on his stomach; Cass sat on his back and gave him neck noogies until he screamed.

That was good for two more weeks for both of us, because Shawn being a butthead wasn't a good enough excuse.

Other than one trip to Crookston, I only saw home and school, and that trip wasn't much fun. I was a foster child, so I had to check in with the Imperium's child services every year. More accurately, Mama and Dad had to, and I had to come along. This was the first time I actually enjoyed the trip because it wasn't home!

All in all, it was early May when we were finally both free to do something, anything, other than visit each other's house.

We were *so* ready!

Saturday arrived, our first day of freedom, and Dad surprised us by offering a trip to Grand Forks for shopping. His 50th wedding anniversary was coming up, and he wanted to pick out something special. Both Cass and I were impressed; we knew fifty years was a big deal. Add the fact we had both outgrown the clothes we had over the winter and were now into the recycled clothes from my older siblings? We said yes so fast he almost didn't finish asking the question!

We didn't have any problem getting over the border, which shouldn't have surprised us. Dad was driving a proper vehicle, not something his slightly impulsive daughter and her best friend put together in a barn. We were behaving, too, at least as much as we ever did. Maybe even a little better. I remember an awful lot of giggles from being somewhere other than home or school for the first time in months.

By the time we got there we were hungry again. Dad couldn't believe it.

"Didn't you have breakfast?" He checked his watch, an old-fashioned one with hands and everything. It was a little after ten.

"Yes, waffles!"

"I had strawberries on mine," said Cass.

"Mama found blueberries for me, and whipped cream!"

"And bacon," Cass added.

"I had bacon too!"

Before we could go into any more detail, he said, "I'm hearing you had breakfast. Here it is, barely ten o'clock, and you're hungry?"

"Yes." There wasn't any other answer. Hungry was hungry.

That's how, instead of going to shop and get home, Dad's stated intention, we ended up at a bakery and getting warm, fresh-from-the-oven rolls and homemade butter.

Our appetites temporarily sated, Dad was permitted to proceed to the next stop: Mama's gift.

He knew we weren't going to have patience to wait while he picked it out *after* we got our clothes. Neither of us were, or for that matter are, clothes hounds. My career as an actress led me to appreciate good clothes, but it didn't come naturally. My other career added a practical layer to my appreciation, but did nothing for my sense of style. Cass was always more comfortable in jeans and a t-shirt, and later a lab coat, than anything else.

We still needed *new* clothes. Stuff which fit and was from the current decade.

I won't say Grand Forks was a great city for shopping, but it was worlds better than Key West. Even though we could get almost anything online we wanted, it simply didn't work for us for clothes. Not then. Not after putting on all those centimeters and kilos. Going by the clothes we were fitting into didn't help, because every manufacturer seemed to use a different sizing system. Stupid. I mean, a girls' ten ought to be the same thing, no matter who made it, right? Nope. Even when it was theoretically the same, it wasn't.

What made the problem worse? We raided my older brothers' childhood clothes. Jeans were jeans, for our age group. A shirt was a shirt. But turning the shirt inside-out to read the tag and seeing it was a boys' six? Not helpful.

Unfortunately, Dad didn't know the first thing about shopping for kids' clothes. You'd be excused for thinking so, having raised his own, but nope. Totally, loveably, and utterly clueless. He brought us first to a discount place, one where you could get a shirt for five Daleys and pants for ten, or a package of a half-dozen socks for two.

Eww.

I'm not a clothes snob, and I've got nothing against *value*. But these things were just gross! Forget about the patterns, which looked like they were done by pouring random colors into the manufacturing plant. No, my problem was the fabric, if you want to call it such. It wasn't cotton, which is what our mothers both preferred us to have. It was some sort of plastic derivative and felt slick to the touch, oily and revolting. The thought of that against my skin?

Eww.

I flatly refused to let Dad buy them, and Cass backed me up. Completely. Full strike.

It sucked for Dad, but we were *not* wearing that stuff. He knew how stubborn we could be, so he sighed and brought us to another store, similar to the first.

Did I mention Dad was a bit of a cheapskate? Maybe value-conscious would be better, but he knew how to squeeze every Daley until Richard the First screamed.

The clothes were a little better but still the same sort of cheap crap.

We said no. Again. With more sighing, and some grumbling, off we went, and he brought us to a thrift store. This was a *major* mistake on his part. Thrifting was like catnip to us, something Mama could have told him if she'd been there.

"Dad, why don't you let us look? You can sit here and rest for a while and we'll bring back anything we like. That way we're all happy." I was being as persuasive as I could, because I was ready to dive in head-first and didn't need Dad holding me back. He was in favor of the plan. He wasn't young, as I may have mentioned, even if he was in good shape. Keeping up with two six-year-old girls was a bit much for him.

"I can wait here."

I kissed his cheek. "Bye!"

We went to the children's clothing section first. Luckily, Dad had brought us to one of the larger thrift stores, so there was a good selection. We found a few things that we'd be happy enough to wear and brought them back to Dad. He looked pleasantly surprised at our speed.

"Done already?"

"No," I said, laughing. "But we don't want to carry it all!"

"Oh." I think he dimly realized the depth of his error, but it was too late. We were gone again.

We didn't go back to the clothing section. Surprised? You shouldn't be. The requirement was met; now it was time to have *fun*.

Cass made a beeline towards the electronics and started rummaging. I stood and watched until she looked at me and said, "Why aren't you helping me?"

"Because you didn't ask. What are you looking for?" I didn't have the slightest idea, so it was a reasonable question.

"I want to make a scanning wide-field telescope."

I still didn't have the slightest idea. "A what?"

She sighed.

"Find anything with a lens," she clarified. "And anything which will turn on its own."

This I could handle.

After about ten minutes we had a pretty significant pile of stuff, which Cass whittled down to a slightly less significant pile. This we brought back to Dad.

"Girls," he started, warningly, face clouding.

"I'll pay for it, Mr. Briggs," Cass said. Our grounding hadn't interrupted our allowances. With both of us grounded we hadn't had anywhere to spend it, so we were both, relatively speaking, rich. At least we felt that way, but a couple hundred Daleys each felt like all the money we could ever need.

It was more than enough for Cass's pile.

The clouds retreated, replaced with curiosity. "I'm sure you can, but why?"

"I'm going to build a scanning wide-field telescope."

Her statement, uttered with her typical complete self-assurance, stopped Dad's protests. I thought it expedient to hit him while he was stunned. "We need to go somewhere else to get clothes, Dad."

"Kendra, they have lots of clothes here." He lifted the not-insubstantial pile we'd accumulated, then waved at the racks.

"We already got the best ones, Dad. The rest are the wrong size or not as nice and comfy."

He had been a diplomat, so knew when to negotiate. "One more store."

"One more," I agreed. I didn't push. Cass was happy with her haul, so I was happy.

After we paid for the bits and pieces and loaded them into the car, Dad finally did what he should have done from the beginning: bring us to a department store. It was Anderson's. I know it doesn't mean anything to you yet because it won't be founded until 2034. Think Macy's, if that helps.

It was the nicest store in the city. Four stories of the finest merchandise you could find in Big Sky, and, for Dad, a place to stash us while he got Mama's gift. Where?

They had a café. Since it was lunchtime, this was a vital consideration. But wait, it gets better!

It.

Was.

Free.

Any customer in the store could go in and get anything they wanted, at no cost to them. It wasn't fancy, just sandwiches and soups and salads and drinks. And ice cream!

Did I mention it was free?

They also had child care. Busy parents could request store staff to stay with their children while they were shopping.

Dad rounded us up, brought us to their child care center, gave them the most strict instructions not to let us out of their sight, and headed off for his shopping.

We went and had lunch and dessert, and then we sat.

I hate waiting; always have.

"Kendra, stop it!"

I was fidgeting and Cass's whisper couldn't have been heard more than, oh, five or six meters away.

"I'm bored!"

She'd never heard that before. She knew me so well; she could see, or maybe sense, my preparation to stand.

"Your dad said to stay here and stay out of trouble!"

"I'm not going to get in trouble!"

And she'd never heard that, either.

"Kendra, come back!"

The minder was adding her voice now, but I completely ignored her, while Cass's words almost made me reconsider.

"I'll be right back," I promised, getting off my seat.

"Kendra Marissa!" I heard, and then Cass tackled me.

You heard right. She *tackled* me!

I went down.

Hard.

I mentioned we went through a growth spurt over the winter and we each gained centimeters and kilos, right?

She gained more, and she was already taller and heavier.

Sometimes life isn't fair.

I hit the floor with a *whump* and a *crack* you could probably hear two floors away.

"Aiyana!" I picked my head up and shouted. "What are you doing?"

She was straddling my back, basically sitting on me, and no matter how I squirmed I couldn't get her loose.

"I'm keeping us out of trouble!" she said.

"Get off me!"

"No! Not until you promise!"

"Fine, I promise!"

"Promise, Kendra! I can see you crossing your fingers!"

I forgot she could see my hands.

I uncrossed them and said, "I promise!"

"You promise what?"

"I promise to behave."

Cass knew better than to let me stop there. "...and?"

Darn. I should have known I wouldn't outsmart her. Maybe I could outstubborn her.

When I didn't continue, she prompted me. "And not run off."

"And not run off, fine, I'll sit and be a good girl. Now will you get off me so I can breathe?"

She did, and she even helped me up.

"Thanks," I said as gracelessly as I ever have.

Cass didn't notice, or at least she didn't pay attention.

"You're welcome. They've got games; you wanna play?"

"No."

"Aw, not board games. They've got full-body immersive VR!"

That was right up my alley. The tackle was forgotten.

"Is it a first person shooter?"

She grinned at me. "Yup."

When Dad showed up an hour later we were still deep in the game, yelling like maniacs and having a great time. We finally surfaced and took off the equipment to find him sitting, watching us fondly and sipping a coffee.

"Did you have fun?" He knew the answer, so he continued with his real question. "Did you stay out of trouble?"

Cass answered before I could indict myself.

"Yes, Mr. Briggs."

"Good. I hoped so. Kendra's mother wasn't certain about bringing you, but I talked her into you coming along. Now, is there anything else you want to do?"

We looked at each other, then said in unison, "One more game!"

Summer Solstice

THE SUMMER WAS SWEET.

We, okay, *I*, seemed to have learned my lesson with the non-incident in the store, and except for the run-of-the-mill stuff we both stayed out of trouble.

I didn't even beat Shawn up more than two or three times and got away with it too because Tammie agreed he was being a snot every single time.

As a reward, we were allowed to stay up for the summer solstice celebration, Litha.

I should back up again. That's the problem with living a life: you forget that other people didn't, and so don't have all the background.

My parents weren't religious, and neither was Charles, Cass's father. Her mother, Tammie, wasn't particularly religious, but she was spiritual if you get the difference. She believed in Earth spirits and fae and various goddesses and gods. There was always something on the little altar they kept by the hearth for someone or another.

I always thought it funny, and Cass was scornful. In retrospect, though, she probably had a pretty profound influence on me. After all, I've ended up calling on the Gods of Olympus a time or two in my life. All her stories of gods got me interested, and I did my own version of research. The

Olympians appealed to me, and I've been gently in their camp ever since. It's hardly what you'd expect from a woman born in the last quarter of the 21st Century!

We learned by osmosis about earth spirits and water spirits and other such beliefs and found them fun. We'd always done the daytime stuff, which mostly consisted of dancing and singing and lots of good food. Maybe there were a couple of invocations, but we'd always been hustled off to my house after dinner and before the big bonfire.

This year?

We were allowed to stay!

We didn't find out until the day before. I suspect they were waiting for us to screw up, but we were still behaving so we were invited. Tammie told us, very solemnly, as befitted a believer.

I was bouncing. Cass was grumpy.

"Superstition," she muttered, and I elbowed her in the ribs. I was *not* going to let her ruin it for me!

"What can we do?" I asked.

Tammie explained, and here I'm afraid I'm going to have to ask you to fill in the blanks for yourself. Her version of paganism or Druidism (I never knew exactly which) is a serious matter for her. I don't want to divulge anything that shouldn't be out there. Since I'm still pretty ignorant about what is and isn't important, I can't say anything.

We prepared, and even Cass started to get into it, pointing out similarities to other ceremonies she'd seen or heard of.

Tammie's pregnancy was showing now, and the baby, a little girl, was kicking up a storm. We could see her little feet pushing against Tammie's skin. I'd never seen anything like it outside of a couple old movies and found it fascinating. I resisted to urge to ask if she'd burst out of Tammie's belly.

Since she was kicking, Tammie had a hard time with all the moving she needed to do. I was recruited to help her, and I have to say I was just about insufferable.

"Look out, getting things for Tammie!"

"Coming through with Tammie's basket!"

"Don't drink all the tea! Tammie needs some!"

A right little snot, I was.

Cass helped too, of course, but I was really into it and she was more tolerant, at best.

Soon enough it was time to light the bonfire.

Charles had built it, with Shawn's help. Shawn was nine that summer and starting to feel like he ought to be more helpful, at least occasionally. Stacking kindling, tinder, and logs was one of the occasions.

We had to wait until a certain time, as the sun touched the western horizon, before lighting it. We weren't standing idle, though. We all had candles, real candles with flame and everything, and Tammie had positioned us most carefully around the fire pit. She walked in a circle, clockwise, I remember, and said, well, things.

Yeah, that's another one of those intentional omissions.

She spoke and walked and watched the sun as it sank lower and lower in the sky. Every so often we were supposed to speak in response to something she said, and I don't think we missed any of our cues.

Charles was on the North point, Cass on the East, I was on South, and Shawn was West. I was swiveling my head, looking all around, but I stopped when I saw Shawn's face.

He was grinning.

Now, I knew that grin. It was one I knew from my face, and it didn't bode well. It meant he'd done something and was waiting for it to pay off.

Normally I would have shouted for Tammie, but I had two problems. I didn't have any idea what he'd done, and Tammie had been most emphatic: we were *not* to leave our spots for *any* reason.

Which meant all I could do was watch him.

Finally, the sun met the horizon, seeming to melt along it, a spreading pool of reddish-orange, and Tammie said, "Now."

This was our signal. All four of us stepped forward, knelt, and touched our candle flames to wicks which led into the bonfire.

I don't know what Tammie treated them with, but the wicks caught immediately and started burning. They hissed and kicked off multicolored flames. I was mesmerized watching it. I'd seen fires, yes, but never green flames, or purple, or that particular shade of blue, and certainly not all the colors at once! I suppose that was the point, but all I knew at the time was it was *pretty*!

I remembered to step back and I tossed a glance at Cass. She seemed to be into it. Then I looked over to Shawn.

The grin was bigger. Whatever was going to happen was about to happen.

I didn't dare move from my point; Tammie was quite clear on the subject. I couldn't yell either. Except for our replies, we weren't supposed to speak.

But Shawn...!

I honestly hadn't the slightest idea what to do.

Then it all became moot.

Suddenly there was a *pop!* and a cloud of sparks.

I didn't jump. I was expecting something. Cass did, and I think it must have been Charles who squeaked.

Why Charles? Because Tammie didn't flinch. She continued her chant.

There was another *pop*, and another. Then they came in rapid succession, more and more sparks jumping with every burst.

With a final *bang*, bigger and louder than all the others, Shawn's little contribution to the evening ended.

The brat was howling with laughter, bent over with his hands on his knees, completely oblivious to his father's silent glare.

Tammie finished up her chant, standing between Charles and the fire, tossed a handful of something into the rising flames, and was on Shawn in three quick steps.

"Shawn Paul Cassidy, you have dishonored the gods and the spirits who protect this home and this family!"

Charles, a half-step behind, added his voice to hers.

Between them they tag-teamed Shawn for ten full minutes.

We found out what he did during the interrogation. Shawn had gotten his hands on fireworks and planted them in the bonfire, undoubtedly when he was helping set it up. It would have been an easy matter for him to light their fuse at the same time as his mother's wick.

Cass and I? We found comfy spots far enough away not to be noticed but close enough to hear everything and enjoyed the show.

Totally worth it.

And the bonfire was pretty, too.

Remodeling

AMAZING EVERYONE, WE stayed out of trouble all summer.

We didn't *try* to stay out of trouble. Then again, even when we got *into* trouble, we never intended it. It always came as a surprise to us, as much as anyone, when one of our ideas blew up in our faces.

Not literally.

Well, not too often, and none of my ideas! I didn't play with chemicals. That was Cass's realm. But we avoided it that summer. We weren't talking about explosions, anyway. The last explosion was caused by Shawn, not us, and boy did he catch it!

But this isn't about him, except when he got in our faces. It's about us.

We weren't grounded any longer, but we didn't have the freedom we had the previous summer. The trike we'd used was dismantled as a consequence of our little at-sea adventure. If it hadn't been, it still would have been too small for us. Our bikes were replaced, but we were enjoined from altering them, with a particular eye to Cass. As a result, they were purely kid-powered.

It wasn't terrible. The area around Key West didn't have any hills worth mentioning. Some number of thousands of years earlier the entire area had been pretty well bulldozed by many ice sheets, flattened and scraped smooth and flattened again. It was, and still is, the southern side of the glacial Lake Agassiz, and no I'm not going to explain it to you in any detail. It's enough to know it was a big damn lake which drained umpteen years ago and dropped a megaton of muck and mud on our part of the Imperium.

This made for great farming and boring landscapes.

Except for the glacial erratics, there weren't any high points which weren't man-made.

Glacial erratic? Okay, I'll explain that one.

A glacial erratic is a boulder that was dropped by a glacier as it retreated. Some of them can be tens of meters tall and wide. They're called erratics because that's what their placement is, erratic. No rhyme or reason to it, just wherever they happened to fall.

The reason this is important? Even though we were reduced to muscle power, getting around was fairly easy in terms of up-and-down. But it was a long, long way to get anywhere interesting. We still went into town every couple of days, but that got old quickly.

What's that?

Bicycle for the sake of bicycling?

Are you seriously offering this as a suggestion?

You've never spent a summer day in Key West. Not that one. I can tell.

How?

If you had, you'd know it gets *hot* there in the summer. Like, melt the tires of the bike to the asphalt if you stay in one place for too long hot, which encouraged us to keep moving.

Or stay home where it's cooler.

So we didn't go out much, at least not during the hottest parts of the day.

It also meant we were shanghaied into helping Cass's folks in redoing their home. Or maybe it's more accurate to say we shanghaied ourselves into the project.

Why were they doing it? The baby.

I didn't understand. Sure, their home was smaller than ours, but it was still good-sized. Four bedrooms, two bathrooms, the usual assortment of other rooms, all on a single floor. Her parents had one room, Cass had one, and Shawn had one. By my math, that left plenty of room for a tiny baby, right?

Well, no.

Apparently not.

See, the spare bedroom was being used as a sort of office space, since both Tammie and Charles worked from home whenever they could. They couldn't give it up, not easily. The other rooms wouldn't work, since they occasionally needed privacy for work things. That meant doors that closed, and their kitchen, living room, and dining room all flowed into each other.

Share with Cass? No. Cass simply refused. From what Cass told me later, they wanted her to give up her space, but she was adamant and eventually got her way.

Which led to them deciding to add to the house.

The decision was to build a really big room, the biggest in the house, with a bathroom attached. This would be the new suite for her parents. The entry to the house would be through their former bedroom, which would now be their office. That allowed the old office to be the baby's room.

Whew!

We thought it was great, because we got to see the construction from the beginning right through the end. Since they needed the space by September at the latest, the workers were there every single day, and it was amazing how quickly it went up! The longest delay was laying the pipes into the concrete foundation and waiting for it to dry.

Now, I didn't have an opinion, or at least not a reasoned opinion, but I did overhear one of the discussions they had with my Dad. This was after the building work was completed, and the new room ready to be moved into. He was helping shift something heavy; a dresser, maybe?

"Isn't Kaeli going to sleep in your room, at least at first?"

They'd decided on Kaeli Almich as the baby's name.

"Yes, it's what we did with Shawn and Aiyana." Charles sort of grunted.

"Why all this work now?" Dad wiped the sweat from his eyes. Summer. Hot, remember?

Charles stopped as well. I think he was happy to. "Well, Tam won't be able to help out soon, and by the time we need the bedroom it'll be the middle of winter."

"But do you really need all this?" Dad waved his hand around.

"If we're going to get anything done with this house, it has to be now, and if we're building, why, we may as well build big!"

"I suppose."

They carried off the whatever-it-was and I didn't hear any more.

Cass and I were often pressed into service, since we were hanging out and trying not to get underfoot. They put us to work moving small things and cleaning and generally making ourselves useful. We even got to help the workers a couple times, once we'd convinced them we knew which end of the power tool to hold.

I totally didn't, but it was pretty easy to figure out and neither of us lost anything important. Cass? She built the trike. She was a dab hand at it.

The summer was fun, in other words. Kinda hard work but fun.

School started in late August, and now we were in Second Grade, which was kinda awkward for Cass. That height thing again, you know? Not only was she taller than all the girls in our grade, she was taller than all the boys except Allen.

This was also the first year she started her advanced classes. After lunch she would get pulled out of homeroom and brought to another class, where she'd learn stuff as fast as she wanted. It was mostly the hard subjects, like math and science. Soft subjects, like English and music and art and history, she learned with the rest of us.

I hated it.

I begged and pleaded with my parents to get me into those classes with her. After a few weeks they finally agreed to talk with the school. I wasn't at the meeting, so I don't know what was said, but about a week later I got pulled out of class did a bunch of tests.

I didn't get in. I found out later, much later, that I very nearly did. My scores were all high but not high enough to qualify me. Between you and me, I think the school wanted to split us up. Wouldn't surprise me if it was true, but there's nobody I can ask any longer so it's kinda a moot point.

September came and went, and now Tammie looked like she was practicing to be the letter b, or maybe p. Sorta a combination of both. Either way, no Kaeli.

The rooms were settled, painting done, all the necessary furniture and supplies laid in for the baby. I didn't have any idea how much work a baby was, or how much they needed to thrive. I asked questions constantly, and learned.

Everything was ready. Except, apparently, Kaeli.

The first week of October went by and still no baby.

All the adults were tense. They tried to hide it, but kid radar picks up on emotions like nobody's business.

If you're empathetic, like Cass is, you try to help. She did, maybe a little too much if you know what I mean.

Shawn, on the other hand, was fully in his patented brat mode. Not only wasn't he getting a brother, but with Kaeli's delayed arrival it currently *wasn't* all about him. He was ten times worse than usual. I thumped him good a couple of times, and it tells you how distracted her folks were that I didn't even get in trouble, even when he ratted me out. Not even the black eye I gave him was sufficient to drag me down. He avoided me as best he could after the second time, so I made sure to stick close to Tammie to give her some peace.

Yup, that's me, the peacemaker. Peace through superior firepower.

Finally, it's late September, and I'm getting nervous, but not because the adults were. No, I had my own reasons. Look, nothing against Kaeli, who turned out to be a lovely, sweet, kind woman, but I didn't want to share my birthday with a baby, even if she wasn't going to be part of my family.

Childhood jealousy. Not fun.

We had a joint birthday celebration on the 28th, and it was somewhat muted. Yes, we had friends, but so much of the focus was on Tammie, sitting in a chair and not doing much, that we felt we missed out. None of our parents were focused on the kids they had, but on the one who was on the way.

The delay had gotten to be too much. On October 2nd, Charles packed Tammie into their car and headed for East Grand Forks and the hospital, promising to be home in a few days with Kaeli. Cass was happy, if a little worried about her parents being gone. She was going to spend the time at my house, and that made up for a bunch. Shawn was miserable for the same reason.

On the 3rd we got a call from the hospital. Dad put it up so we could all see it, and there she was, all small and red and wrinkly and unhappy with the entire situation: Kaeli. Tammie looked tired but happy. Charles stayed out of sight. Cass and I wandered away pretty soon, Shawn having left way earlier, utterly unimpressed with his new sister. We stuck around long enough to find out they'd all be home in two days, which is probably where Cass got her idea.

See, she thought it would be a good surprise to decorate Kaeli's new room.

I had questions. "Uh, Cass? Didn't we already do this?"

We had. It was one of the things we'd helped with over the summer. Not to be sexist or anything, but Tammie had wanted a traditional girl's room, which meant pink and frills and soft fuzzy toys all over.

Cass had other ideas.

"We did, but we can do it better. Come on."

I was reluctant, but hey, this was *Cass*. I was gonna follow her and help.

She'd been clever, which wasn't a surprise. There were packages and boxes all organized in her room, ready to go.

"What is all this?"

"Stuff I liked when I was little." She lifted a package and headed out of the room.

I grabbed another and followed. "How little?"

"Three. I figure it'll give Kaeli a nice head start. I'll bet she's going to be smart, like me."

"Nobody's smart as you," I muttered, still stinging from the school's tests, but I kept following.

Once we got to the room, Cass asked me to keep bringing things in for her while she unpacked and started putting things up. I was perfectly prepared to do this since I didn't have a clue what her plan was.

Over the next hour, I carted everything from one room to the other. Cass took stuff out and put it up as fast as I carried it in, and when I brought the last bag she said, "Almost done."

I looked around.

It *was* Cass's room, at least as nearly as my early memories could recall.

"Um. Cass?" I tried to figure out how to say what I was feeling, that a newborn baby wasn't going to need terminals and robots and a chemistry set and all the other stuff which thrilled Cass.

She turned to me with a big, hopeful smile on her face, and my resolve crumbled.

"It's perfect," she said, and all I could do was nod. "Mom's going to be so surprised!"

"I think so," I agreed.

Cass was a hundred percent right.

Roommates

WHEN KAELI CAME HOME, Cass was nearly bursting with excitement. I'm sure Tammie's first thought was pleased, because here was the Big Sister acting all happy and cheerful about the Baby Sister coming home, and to an extent it was true. Cass had, over the summer, come to look forward to her new role.

But it was the redecoration which was her pride and joy. When Tammie put Kaeli down for a nap in the crib in their bedroom, Cass practically dragged her along the hallway to Kaeli's room.

I don't know what Cass said; I was busy.

Doing what?

Thumping Shawn.

He was being a snot again, and since I had taken on official Shawn-thumping duties, well, my mandate was clear. He got a good pounding, then I followed him until he barricaded himself in his room. My job done, I went in search of Cass.

By then Cass had finished giving Tammie the tour of the new and improved room. Her mom stood there, looking stunned. Eventually she forced a smile and said, "You put in a lot of hard work. Are you sure you want Kaeli to have all this?"

I think she was trying to find a way out, but Cass didn't give her the out she wanted.

"I'm sure, Mom. I'll even show her how to use it all!"

"That's great," quavered Tammie. "It might be a while before she's ready."

"It's okay. It doesn't have to be today." Her enthusiasm shone through.

Well, even I could tell Cass had a skewed idea of how quickly Kaeli was going to be doing anything. She was cute, sure, in a pink-and-wrinkled sort of way, but she didn't do much. I didn't know what to do, so I did the only thing I could.

"Cass, let's go over my house for a while. I think Kaeli's sleeping."

Tammie jumped on this. "What a good idea, Kendra. Yes, Kaeli needs her sleep. She's very little and is going to be sleeping a lot."

Off to my house we went.

That established a pattern for the next weeks, one I found strangely fulfilling. We'd play at her house until Kaeli woke. Cass would help with feeding or changing as much as her mom would allow, then we'd go back to my house when Tammie had enough help.

Cass was a good Big Sister. She loved Kaeli, right from the start, and she learned how to play with her and talk to her and make goofy faces at her in a way Kaeli could process. Kaeli, for her part, went from a squalling lump to almost-a-person pretty quickly, and Tammie was always quick to credit Cass for her role in it. But Cass got bored after a while, since Kaeli was, after all, an infant.

What was especially tough on Cass was the location of Kaeli's room: down the hall from her.

Now, down the hall might not sound bad, and in many ways it wasn't. There was a reason. Her parents wanted Cass close when she was little, just like they now wanted Kaeli close so they could hear her at night.

The problem arose because, as a child, Cass always wanted her door to be open. Always.

I'd argue with her to close it when I slept over, because more than once we got in trouble for being too loud and waking up her parents. Sometimes she'd give in, sometimes I would. But her preference was always open.

Now, I don't know how familiar you are with babies' sleep habits. I wasn't at all, back then, because, well, only child in the house. Cass didn't know either.

Basically, they don't, or at least it seems that way.

Babies will wake up for any reason, or none at all.

Need changing.

Need feeding.

Gassy.

Whatever the cause, in my experience an infant is up roughly every ninety minutes from birth until about three months before it gradually stretches out.

With our kids, it didn't bother me. I've never needed much sleep, thanks to my wonky genetics, so catching a number of naps overnight worked. When Cass was nursing it was tougher, but we planned ahead. At least one of the feedings during the overnight would be a bottle Cass put aside earlier so she could catch at least one solid stretch.

But that's for later.

Back in the day, Cass needed her sleep. Nine hours, by preference. Eight at a minimum. Ten if she could get it.

With Kaeli in the house, she was getting six or seven hours, interrupted, which meant she was getting crankier and crankier as the days went on. Cass was always the happier of the two of us. Her temperament was bright and cheerful and optimistic, from the moment she woke up to the end of the night.

But with the lack of sleep she started losing the shine. She was still sweet with Kaeli, but everyone else? She wasn't any fun to be around.

She got into fights at school! Yes, *fights*, as in more than one! It looked like it might even interfere with our Halloween plans, that's how bad it got. A few weeks on, and the third note home from her teachers, her parents and mine had a hasty meeting.

"Kendra," Dad said after they finished. "Aiyana is going to be staying with us for a while."

"Thank you!" I said, wrapping my arms around him. "Best Dad ever!"

He patted between my shoulders, then told me to go clean my room. My argument, that she'd seen it plenty of times before and in worse condition than it was in now, didn't work. My heart wasn't in it, though, because Cass was coming to stay!

A couple hours later she arrived, with two bags: one full of her school books, one full of the computers and electronics she couldn't deal without. Oh, and a towel. She never forgot her towel. Charles followed with a bag of clothes.

This was, um. Let me think.

Wednesday. October 29.

Friday was Halloween. And boy oh boy, did we have plans!

We were definitely going to make this year the best.

Halloween.
Ever.

Nothing Ever Happens on Halloween

WE DIDN'T PLAN ANYTHING big for Halloween.

Right.

If you believe that, I've got some tropical property for you on Titan.

We always loved Halloween, and the restrictions the school imposed after the events of the previous year just meant we needed to be more concentratedly creative. The fact that Kaeli had arrived hadn't slowed us in the slightest. I don't want you to think we only started getting ready the day Cass moved over to my house because of Kaeli. We'd started planning in the summer.

I wanted to go old school, and by that I mean my fave pop culture. She could be Black Widow, even though I really dug the character, and I was going to be Carol Danvers for most of the day before ending the day decked out as Captain Marvel. I thought we could have all sorts of fun kicking bad guy butts all day long.

Cass disagreed.

She was on a reading kick.

Well, okay, fair point; she was *always* on a reading kick. Over the summer she'd gotten into the classics. Like, classic-classics. Nineteenth-century and earlier classics. I think her dad was to blame, but wherever she'd started it, she'd discovered Mary Shelley. She devoured "Frankenstein, or The Modern Prometheus," and that was it. Her plans for Halloween were set, and there was no budging her. Cass wanted to go as a scientist and me as her creation, sort of a Frankensteinian monster.

I tried to argue, I did! I mean, I'd seen *Young Frankenstein*, and I knew I wasn't tall, or bald, and I knew I couldn't tap dance. Besides, I was shorter than Cass; how could I be the monster?

My logic didn't work on her, and I couldn't persuade her to do the comic book thing, either. So it would be Aiyana the Mad Scientist, and Kendra the Monster.

We didn't have any trouble with the costumes. All she needed was a crazed look, which she practiced for hours in the mirror with critiques by yours truly, and a lab coat. She spent a bunch of time trying to figure out what sort of tools a mad scientist would carry in her coat pockets, and tried to talk her Dad into getting her a laser scalpel. Fortunately for everyone, he refused. She settled on a stethoscope, one of those reflectors doctors wear mounted in the middle of their foreheads that makes them look like a Cyclops, some scissors, and a few big needles.

My costume was almost easier, and it was all Cass. I had no idea about the Bride of Frankenstein with the black hair and white stripes, at least not until Cass explained it to me. Now that I think of it, though, how did *she* know? It's not in the original novel, it was a Hollywood invention. Huh. She must have been going through old movies to get an idea of things too!

Mama found some of the old clothes I had pretty well turned into rags and I was done. Well, not quite. She had to dye my hair and then tease it upwards, something I had a really tough time with because I didn't like sitting still that long.

She had to do it twice: once for practice, and then again the day of. To be fair, she did the dye the night before, and only had to do the teasing in the morning, which made it a little better.

My hair? Oh, you mean my habitual pixie cut. I hadn't started getting a voice in the whole this is how your hair will be cut debate, so it was pretty long. I kept it long until high school, then went through the usual teen experimentation before letting it grow out again. It wasn't until I was in OutLook that I settled on my pixie look.

The tough part about what we planned to do was the role reversal. At school and with friends, I was usually the ringleader and Cass was the cheerleader and support. This time *she* had to take the lead. She was the creator, and I was just the monster. We had to come up with a way to convince everyone of this.

After bouncing ideas off each other for days, we settled on a plan. She would take the lead, acting like she was having problems controlling her creation. I'd start the day docile, but get more and more inquisitive and aggressive as the day went on, lunging at other students. Cass was supposed to try to restrain me, whatever way she could manage it.

I didn't plan to make it easy. We had friends to terrify!

Friday, Halloween, finally arrived, and we rode to school. On the bus ride I didn't do much, just growled and glared at the other students while Cass told me to behave. I would, but

I'd give her a glare when her back was turned. Every eye was on me, and I loved it.

Once we arrived at school and got inside, the fun really started.

I took off my heavy coat, mittens, and boots – it was snowing, I remember, not an unusual occurrence for Halloween, and I had no desire to be cold – and started prowling the halls before we had to get to homeroom. Cass chased me for a while, doing her best truly terrible German accent and ordering me to "Come back!"

Well, it escalated all morning. In the classes I behaved, more or less, not wanting to see the principal so early in the day. Between classes? I turned it up a notch, really testing the limits. Cass was having fun, too, as her muffled giggles attested.

Then came lunch. By that point I was being so unruly Cass had resorted to the dog collar and leash. We made a point of showing how much I hated having it on, how strongly I was resisting it, and the effort it took Cass to keep me from breaking loose.

It was great!

I swear, the kids were eating it up, and the teachers were as well. At least two of them were calling encouragement to Cass, so I made sure to give a good lunge at them to see if they'd jump.

One did.

But – and this was the key to our whole plan – after lunch, Cass and I went to different classes.

I went back to my class, still wearing the collar, the leash dangling down. It was art, and one of my favorites, so I didn't do too much. I limited myself to a few growls when kids got too close, and one kinda vicious almost-bark when Barry tried to pick up the leash.

Not a good idea.

Other than that, I behaved. Hey, like I said, it was one of my favorite classes, and I didn't want to screw it up!

The next class was social studies. Yuck. Which meant I didn't feel any need to restrain myself.

I had fun with it.

I started off quietly, though my classmates were keeping wary eyes on me. As the class went on I got more fidgety and started to eye my nearest seatmates in a way guaranteed to make them nervous. You ever see a seven-year-old try to shuffle one of those school desks without being obvious? Pretty soon there was an empty circle around me that extended about a meter in any direction.

I climbed down from the desk and started sort of shuffling around, dragging the leash, and being really *really* inquisitive. I got right up in their faces, looking over their shoulders, looking up from under their arms.

Lots of giggling was going on from the kids who were watching my antics, but the one I was paying attention to? They were locked on me.

I did my best not to disappoint. I think I was probably channeling more Gollum than Bride, but the point wasn't accuracy, it was menace and scaring them.

I succeeded.

By the end of the class the space around my desk had expanded to three meters. In a twist which I now find funny but didn't appreciate as a seven-year-old, my classmates had to put their desks back while I shuffled out.

There was only one class left in the day before I reunited with Cass, so I had to go big before I went home. The problem was it was the same teacher we'd had when things went bad last year, Mr. Temba.

This was going to take diplomacy.

Fortunately, I was Dad's girl. He'd survived decades in the Imperium's Foreign Service, and I learned from him. One lesson I remembered was to get your position in first, so I made sure I was the first one to arrive at the class.

"Hi, Mr. Temba," I said, strolling into the room, behaving perfectly appropriately.

"Kendra." He ignored the dragging leash and ragged clothes.

"I had a question?"

"What is it, Kendra?"

"Since it's Halloween and all and I'm playing the Bride of the Monster, could I have some fun with the other kids? I'm not going to do anything bad, just sorta walk around and growl a little. I promise not to stab anyone."

See? Diplomatic.

Fortunately for me, Mr. Temba was a soft touch, and his class was the last of the day. He smiled and said, "Sure, Kendra. But don't bite, either. Deal?"

"Deal!"

I went and sat at my desk and waited. I didn't have to wait long; I might have been first to the class, but I wasn't first by much.

My activities in the afternoon had gotten around, apparently, and I received a bunch of side-eye stares and wary glances. I kept things quiet as class started. I wanted to get them to forget about the Monster in their midst.

After ten minutes or so I decided to ramp it up. I prowled around, sniffing at my classmates. I licked a few, loving the shivers it brought. A couple of the girls actually squealed in surprise.

Of course, that only encouraged me more.

I crept around, and Mr. Temba gave up on trying to teach. I think he was enjoying it almost as much as I was.

With a few minutes left in the class the door burst open. I was irritated with having the spotlight stolen, but choked back the growl that threatened to escape.

"What's going on here!" demanded Mr. Temba. There were probably a dozen kids, older kids, third- and fourth-graders, and most of them ignored him, focusing on me. One, apparently the spokesman, went up to Mr. Temba and said something. I missed the exchange, because I was watching the others. I didn't like how they were looking at me. It was entirely too serious for my taste.

With a hint of nerves, I said, "Uh. Guys?"

"Don't make trouble, Monster," one answered.

I sagged back, relieved. They were in on the game, so I'd play along.

"It's okay, Mr. Temba."

It wasn't.

Nothing Ever Happens on Halloween 2

THIS WAS GETTING OLD, fast.

"Where are we going?"

They had surrounded me and wrapped a rope around my arms, pinning them to my side, and led me from the class. I didn't fight, didn't protest, except for a few token growls. I learned, see? But now we were in the hallway, and I figured I ought to know what was going on, so I asked again.

"Guys?"

Still no answer.

"Okay, ha-ha, this is fun and all, but really. Where are we going?"

Nothing, so I wriggled in the bonds. Too tight to get out of. I tried to stop, but they dragged me along with the end of the rope.

"This isn't fun anymore!" I yelled in the deserted corridor. Deserted? Yes. The school had been built decades earlier, at a time when the local population needed lots of space. Over the years, the number of kids had shrunk. It didn't make sense to build a new school, so as they needed less space they condensed the footprint they used. There were a couple wings that were virtually abandoned, and this was one of them.

"Quiet. You don't want to get in trouble again," one of the boys said.

He had a point, blast it.

Everyone in school knew about the disaster that was Halloween last year. Worse, everyone knew I was the reason for the ban on costumes this year. I don't know if this played any role in my current situation, but the fact remained: I was trouble on Halloween.

I stayed quiet and shuffled along.

This part of the school I didn't know. Not really a surprise, because although all the students from Pre-K through 6th were in the same building we had our own areas. We mixed at lunch and some of the art and gym classes, but the academic subjects and homerooms were all separated. This wing was creepy, dark and deserted. No kids anywhere, no noise. Eventually, we stopped at a door. It was pulled open, revealing an empty classroom, and I was shoved inside, my arms still bound.

"Hey!" I protested, but the door was pushed closed.

"Great," I muttered, plopping down in a chair. "Just great."

I don't know how long I was in there alone. There was a clock, but like the lights, it wasn't working. I don't think it was more than thirty minutes, or less than twenty. After this timeless period, the door opened again, letting less-gloomy light into the near-dark.

"You created her. You're going to burn with her!" is what I heard, and then Cass was pushed through. She was trussed up like me and didn't look any happier about it.

Then what they said hit me.

Burn?

Oh, crap. That couldn't possibly be good. They had to be kidding, right?

The door had slammed closed again before I could react, so I turned my attention to Cass.

"What did you *do?*" she demanded, stomping over to me, fury on her face.

Okay, this was unexpected.

"I didn't do anything!"

"Then why did those goons grab me out of my class and say I was gonna pay for what *you* did?"

"I don't know! They grabbed me out of my classroom too!"

"*What did you do?*" She was almost yelling, the anger making her voice hoarse.

"*Nothing!*" I shouted back.

She took a half-step back and regarded me.

"Nothing?"

"No! Well," I amended. "I was playing the Monster in my classes, you know? Growling, and sniffing at kids, just like we planned it."

"Uh-huh." If she'd been untied, her arms would have been crossed, I could tell.

"But I didn't do anything bad, not that would make anyone do this! And besides, none of them are in our grade!"

That caught her attention.

"None?"

"Nope."

I could see her brain engaging, her irritation set aside by curiosity. "Why did they grab us?"

"I don't know. I thought they were playing, but they seemed pretty serious about it with the ropes and all. Did you hear what they said?"

"Not really," she admitted. "I was kinda mad."

"They were talking about burning us."

"What?!"

Even though I rarely knew something Cass didn't, I didn't feel good about this tidbit. "Yeah, you because you created me, and me because I'm playing the Monster, I guess."

Her pale face went ashen.

"That's not good."

"No." I wholeheartedly agreed with her. "Really not good. What do we do?"

"We'd better get out of these ropes," she said.

"How?"

It was a fair question. My hands were totally bound up, and so were hers. All that were free were the tips of my fingers. Fingertips. Hmm. Maybe...

"Turn around?"

"Why?" asked Cass, but she was already spinning.

"I want to see how they did this."

"Oh."

I bent over, peering through the murkiness. Yup. They tied her, too. I could see the knot, but I didn't have the first idea what it was or how I could undo it without my hands.

"Crap."

"Kendra!" Cass sounded shocked.

"What? Oh. Sorry." I had forgotten her parents didn't curse. Like, at all. Mine didn't, much, but Dad let slip the occasional colorful word, and Mama, well. She once hit her thumb with a hammer, hanging up a picture, and I don't think she stopped swearing for a good two minutes. It was educational.

"Can you come over here, then bend down? I'll see what I can do."

She did, awkwardly leaning down and rolling until I could touch the knot with my fingertips. I fiddled with it for a few minutes before sighing.

"I can't get a grip," I grumped. Cass peered around the room. I didn't know what she was looking for, so I asked.

"I don't know where we are," she said. "If we were in the art room, there's all sorts of things I could use to get us out."

I looked too, but the dark didn't give up its secrets. The only light to speak of was coming from the window in the door. The door. What about the door?

It had a doorknob, and I had the beginning of a rotten idea. "Cass?"

"What?" She'd moved over to one of the countertops and was examining it.

"I think we can open the door."

She spun around. "What did you say?"

"I think we can open the door. If we stand on a box or something I'll be tall enough to get my fingers on one side of the knob, and you can turn the other side."

She was looking for a box before I finished talking.

"I've got it!" Cass started kicking at something at the back of the room, knocking it towards the door. I eagerly stood and helped her. It looked like it used to hold water bottles, maybe. In the bottom there were circular indentations a half-dozen centimeters across, thirty centimeters tall, and maybe half the size of a desktop.

It was perfect, if it would hold our weight.

We pushed it into place.

"Ready?"

"How are we doing this?"

"What do you mean?"

"I'm right-handed, so are you."

I hadn't considered this. In my mind, we stood back-to-back and used whichever hand was closest.

"Oh. Um. I'll get up first, face the edge of the door, then you stand behind me?"

"Suits."

We climbed up and into position.

"Ready?"

I felt her nod before she said, "Yes."

"I'll push up, you push down."

I adjusted my fingers, and said, "On three. One, two, three."

We twisted our fingers and the knob...turned!

The door slid out, gloriously open. We jumped off the crate and ran as best we could, a little unbalanced with our arms secured.

"Now what?" panted Cass. Running was hard when tied up.

"Homeroom."

"Then?"

I didn't have much of a plan, so I faked it. "Then we get out of these ropes and go home!"

We were in the part of the school we knew, and almost back to our homeroom, when we ran into a problem in the form of another closed door.

By now I didn't care about anything other than getting help and out of the ropes, so I kicked the door, waited, then kicked again. I have *never* been so happy to see an angry teacher than I was at that moment!

Ms. Simmons's expression turned from anger to concern when she saw us through the window. We backed up so she could open the door.

"Kendra? Aiyana? What's going on?"

We didn't answer until we we'd pushed through the doorway into the safety of the classroom.

"Some boys were playing a stupid game," I said before Cass could answer with more truth than we could explain. "We didn't want to play anymore."

Which was true enough, if not the entire truth.

"Why are you tied up?"

"It was part of their game," Cass added. "Can you untie us, please?"

It wasn't until she'd untied us that I noticed we were the only ones in the room.

"Where is everyone?" I asked Ms. Simmons.

"Didn't you hear the bell?" she said. "School ended fifteen minutes ago."

"Oh, crap."

Nothing Ever Happens on Halloween 3

"KENDRA SMITH!"

"Sorry, Ms. Simmons." I'd forgotten we were still in school, but honestly I didn't think of it. Somehow the wrath of my homeroom teacher didn't seem quite as daunting as it had at the beginning of the day.

"I don't like to hear that sort of language, young lady."

"Yes, Ms. Simmons." I managed to put some contrition into it this time, and she went back to tidying up with only a sniff.

"We missed the bus," Cass almost whispered.

"Exactly." I kept my voice low, too.

"Do you think..." She didn't need to finish the thought.

"If I was them? Yeah."

"Why?" She sounded offended. "It's a stupid game, right?"

"I don't think they're playing anymore."

"What?" she squeaked.

"Shh!" I swiveled to look at Ms. Simmons, who was buried in her work. "Remember, I heard them talking about burning us?"

She sobered. "Oh."

"Yeah. Oh. Now, I don't know if they can manage it, but I don't want to find out what they *can* do. It won't be good, and there's lots more of them than us."

"What are we gonna do?"

"Call home? Get someone to pick us up?" I was out of good ideas, so I fell back on prepared positions.

Cass shook her head. "Mom and Dad took Kaeli to a checkup today and won't be back until dinnertime."

"And I'm supposed to stay with you; Mama has a conference and Dad's going with her this weekend." I turned my head and raised my voice. "Ms. Simmons?"

She looked up from cleaning. "Yes, Kendra?"

"I know we missed the bus, but is there another one?"

"Normally, yes, but not today. The late driver isn't feeling well."

"Oh."

"Is there a problem, Kendra?"

"Um. Well, kinda? We were supposed to take the bus, like usual, but we missed it? And we don't know how we're going to get home."

"That is a problem," Ms. Simmons said. "What were you doing that made you miss the bus?"

Oh, crap. Rat out the boys who did this? Or try to keep it quiet?

No-brainer.

"You know those ropes you helped us with? It wasn't really a game," I started to explain. Over the next few minutes, Cass and I managed to get the whole story out, her part, my part, and then together. Halfway through, when Ms. Simmons finally began to take us seriously, she started writing it down, asking us for descriptions and all the details we could provide, which dragged it out even longer. At the end, though, she was as pale as milk and looking scared.

Okay, scared wasn't what I wanted, but at least it was an adult taking us seriously.

She pressed a button on her desk. I didn't know her desk had buttons, and was even more surprised when I heard the principal.

"Yes, Ms. Simmons?" He didn't sound happy.

"Miss Smith and Miss Cassidy are in my classroom."

"They missed their bus?"

"Yes, but that's not the issue. Do you have a few minutes?"

He hesitated, then said, "Yes, of course."

"We'll be down in a moment."

I didn't want to leave the classroom. I know it may come as a surprise to you, sitting there and reading this, but while I might have been impulsive and maybe even a bit foolhardy at times, I wasn't stupid. One-on-one, or two-on-one? No problem. Three-on-one? Probably not a problem, but I'd think about it first.

Eight-on-one? Nine-on-one? No way. I wanted an adult, and I was not going to let Cass out of my sight.

We gathered our belongings, put on our coats, then I took Cass's hand. "We're ready."

Ms. Simmons looked grim but determined. I noticed she locked the door to her classroom on our way out. This was not exactly encouraging. Together we marched down the hallway. I was pivoting my head, straining my ears and peering into every corner. I didn't think they'd try to jump us, not with a teacher right there, but I wasn't taking any chances.

We made it to the principal's office without any incident, but I still waited until the door closed behind us to release Cass's hand.

She grabbed it right back when we saw the principal.

He was sitting at his desk, but other than that there was nothing normal about the scene. Gone was his usual suit and tie, gone was his slicked-back grey hair, gone was the stern-but-fair man who I'd gotten to know all-too-well in the past two-plus years. Instead, I was facing...

Well, to be honest, I wasn't sure who I was facing. His hair was black, though still styled in the usual way. His eyes were bright yellow, almost cat-like. His skin was red, and I could see much of it, as he was only wearing a cape...a cape? Yes, a cape, and a pair of tight knee-length shorts. He was holding what looked like a pitchfork, though I found out later it was supposed to be a trident, and were those two small black horns coming from his forehead? Why yes. Yes, they were.

Cass screamed!

He hurried around the desk, saying, "Miss Cassidy, please, it's me!" Cass backed frantically away from him. I don't think the feet helped. Instead of his polished black loafers, he wore what looked like giant goat feet, hairy and nasty, which extended up to his shorts.

I admit, the feet gave me a start, and I might have yelped. Just a little bit.

"It's my costume!" he said, frustration coming through, and I took a closer look.

Same nose.

Same mouth.

Same ears.

Same voice.

Okay, maybe it was the principal. We were in his office. Ms. Simmons wouldn't bring us here if this was an imposter, and she wasn't freaking out. But wow, he looked different. And who knew adults liked to dress up too?

I asked the first question that popped into my head.

"Aren't you going to be cold?" Minnesota, remember? It was going down below zero that night, *way* below, and there was snow on the ground already.

He smiled, which was a bit disturbing. Smiling? At me? I *never* got to see him smile; our relationship wasn't built that way.

"Thank you for your concern, Miss Smith," he said. "Do you think you can stop screaming now, Miss Cassidy?"

"You look like the devil!"

Devil? Oh. Well, yeah. I guess so. My folks weren't particularly religious, and Cass's mom was some sort of pagan. I'd picked up enough to know some people believed in a God and a Devil, but I hadn't the slightest idea what either would look like.

"Yes, Miss Cassidy," he was saying. "But it's not real." He picked up a tissue and rubbed a small spot on his arm, which returned to its normal pale color. "See?"

She was beginning to recover her composure. "Sorry for screaming," she muttered.

"And I'm sorry for not warning you, but I was a bit rushed. Now, please, sit down. Tell me what's going on."

As he sat, something magical happened: it was as if the red paint and horns all disappeared, and he was The Principal again, suit and all.

We told him, beginning to end.

"Ms. Simmons, can you confirm any of this?"

"That what they told me," she said. "They were bound in ropes when they came back to the room, which I had to undo. They couldn't have done it by themselves."

He nodded sagely. "Someone tied them up, for reasons we don't know."

"To burn us!" I interrupted.

"As you say, Miss Smith. I don't disbelieve you," he hastened to add. "But it's rather a difficult story to accept. Still, we need to get you home safe. Ms. Simmons, I hate to impose, but can you transport them?"

She was already standing. "I just need to get my coat and turn off the lights."

"Fine. Bring your car around to the front, then call me directly. I'll escort them out to you." She nodded and left. "Girls, Ms. Simmons will take you home, but you're going to wait here with me until she's ready. Would you like some candy?"

He opened a drawer and pulled out a half-empty bowl, obviously left over from the day's festivities. I never met a candy I didn't like, and reached eagerly, but Cass waited until I'd popped the first one into my mouth before taking one of her own.

"Go on," he urged. "If you don't take them, all I'll do is eat them all next week. Probably be gone by the end of Monday."

That was all the prompting we needed, and we loaded up.

Okay, so it's weird, but the next few minutes are one of my favorite memories of school, despite everything which had happened. Just Cass and I in the principal's office, munching on candy, and waiting to get out of school without being grabbed by a bunch of murderous third- and fourth-graders. Strange, eh?

Soon, his phone rang.

"Yes?" Pause. "Good. We'll be right out."

He stood. By now the red skin seemed totally normal to us and we didn't blink, even when he picked up the trident. "Let's go."

We went out first, scanning up and down the hallways but feeling a bit more confident than earlier. The walk took *forever*, but finally we could see the front doors and Ms. Simmons's car beyond, headlamps shining in the encroaching night, and we broke into a run. Candy or no, we wanted to get *home*.

"Girls!" he yelled, but we didn't stop and hit the doors with a bang. They flew open, the cold air hit us, and then my blood froze.

"You didn't think you'd get away, did you?"

It was a kid's voice, yes, and one trying to sound more adult than it was, but I knew it. The last time I'd heard it, it was talking about burning us.

Stupidly, we skidded to a halt instead of barrelling toward the car, only a few more meters away.

"I knew you'd have to leave eventually," he said. "It was just a question of waiting."

In the darkness beyond the sweep of the school's lighting I could see the forms of the others. Crap on toast. I dropped my bag and shucked off my coat. They weren't going to take me down without a fight this time.

"Grab the—"

"*What is the meaning of this?*" The angry bellow blasted them backwards a step, I'd swear to it. I knew the bellow from long experience and flattened myself on the ground, dragging Cass with me. I turned to watch.

With the light from the doors behind him, blotting out the details of his face, I could half-believe our Principal was the Devil. The cloak, so silly-looking in the office, flapped and billowed about him. He held the trident so all of them, and none in particular, were menaced. He strode forward so he was next to us, giving me a closer look than I ever wanted at those goat's feet.

"*They are mine!*" he shouted, waving the trident and forcing them back a few more steps. "*Find your own sacrifice to the gods of the night!*"

Gods of the night? Maybe he was taking this a little bit too seriously. Then he stage-whispered to us, "Get to the car."

Cass was up and running in an instant, and I only lagged behind to snag my coat and bag. Ms. Simmons had watched for the few seconds the entire encounter consumed, frozen, but now opened the rear door. Cass dove in first. I piled on top of her and pulled the door closed with a foot.

"Go!" I don't know which of us said it, maybe both, but we were moving before the door latched shut. I scrambled up and turned, trying to see what was going on behind us. The boys had all scattered, disappearing into the night. All that remained was our principal. His cloak still flapped, but the trident was resting easy as he looked around.

I think he got a kick out of it. As we turned out of the parking lot, I saw him returning to the school and whatever his plans were for the night.

The rest of the evening was anticlimactic. Between the candy we'd gotten and the excitement, we didn't feel like going out. Instead we sat in Cass's room, watching classic movies like *The Mummy* way too late and chomping.

We didn't tell any of our parents.

What happened after? Well, unfortunately the boys were clever. We knew there were cameras all over the school, but they managed to avoid clear shots, so not even the facial recognition software could identify them. The principal was forced to act like it hadn't happened.

It suited us fine. While the school never caught 'em, that didn't mean we couldn't look into it. We had plenty of friends in that school, and sooner or later someone would blab.

But that's a story for another time.

A Puppy?

"WHAT DO YOU WANT FOR Christmas, Kendra?"

Dad always asked me after the Harvest Festival, and I always had a list. I knew the routine.

What about Santa, you say?

Cass told me, proved to me, there wasn't a Santa, all the way back when we were four. It sort of ruined things for my folks. I think they enjoyed playing the role of Santa one more time. Dad adapted to the new situation, and after that I pretty much knew I'd get what I wanted, or at least something close to it.

Each year, when he approached me, I was ready, and this year was no different. He took the sheet of paper I'd carefully written everything on and considered it like he was examining a draft treaty.

See, there were rules to the list. It couldn't be all toys. That was rule number one.

Rule number two was it couldn't all be clothes. Now, when I was little this wasn't an issue. Clothes were something I had to have, not something I craved. A need, practical at the core, and I wore them because it was expected and it was Minnesota and cold more often than not. When I got to be a teenager, I understood the necessity for this rule. Not that I appreciated it, but I understood it.

There had to be practical items on there, things which would be useful to me. If I needed a new tablet because the old one was too old to function, I could put it on there. If I needed new tires for my car, which I did when I was seventeen, I could put them on there. That was rule number three.

Oddly enough, there wasn't a limit on cost. In part it was because my folks didn't worry about money, but they also wanted to capture some of the magic associated with the season.

Rule number four, I had to give Dad the list, not Mama. Why? I don't know, but it was an inviolate rule. If I tried to hand it to Mama she wouldn't even touch it. Rule number five was a killer. Once I gave Dad the list, it was final, no adding allowed. If I forgot something I had to wait. "Must not have been that important," Dad would say. And the final rule was I had to have the list ready when Dad asked for it, which could be any time after the Harvest Festival. He'd remind me before the holiday, but that was it.

I always put a few things on there for Cass, at least until I had enough money to get them myself. She always did the same for me. Our gifts followed the same rules as my parents' list: something fun, something practical, and then there'd be a piece of clothing we wanted the other to have.

Thinking back on it, the clothes seem a little bit silly. I mean, what was mine was hers and what was hers was mine, at least in terms of clothing. We shared everything, absolutely everything, so eventually what I got she wore and vice versa.

Anyway, about a week after the Festival, Dad asked. I raced to my room, grabbed the list, and brought it back. He took it and examined it minutely.

"Hmm," Dad finally said. "Looks fairly comprehensive. I think you're forgetting something, though."

I snatched the paper back, mortified. "No," I said. "I didn't miss anything." I hadn't. This was at least the sixth version of the list since September.

"Are you sure, pumpkin?"

Now I had to wonder. Could I have missed something? Was it possible? I mean, my list started the day after we unwrapped everything, and I added and subtracted all year long. I was really, really careful with it, too, with the whole no adding rule.

"Something you've wanted for a long time?" he added as a hint.

I was still stumped.

Something I wanted for a long time?

Well. Huh.

In terms of *things*, nothing leapt to mind. I didn't *need* anything, and I learned early to be upfront about asking for what I wanted. I'd either get it, or I wouldn't, whether it was a holiday or not. If I didn't get it there was no point in asking again unless it was something age-related, a pretty small category. And if I still wanted it, well, I could save my Daleys.

I didn't want a sibling. For one thing, I had Cass. She was better than a sister could ever be. For another, she had Shawn, and now Kaeli, so I could go hang out with them. Shawn was good for tormenting, and if I had the desire to be babbled at there was Kaeli. She was only about seven weeks old and she was already getting good at it.

Wait.

Could it be...?

There was one thing I'd wanted for years; craved, really.

I wanted a puppy. Yes, I had a cat, or maybe the cat had me. Ownership was always a question with Luna Sassypaws. She was in the house before I was, and viewed me as an interloper with benefits. Chief among them was my willingness to let her sleep in my bed.

But I wanted a dog.

Yeah, yeah, you can lecture me about cliches and all that. I wanted a puppy, and had for years and years. Cass's folks had a working farm, remember? Lots of animals. But no dogs. There were cats, of course, barn cats and ratters and there were always kittens underfoot. I appreciate cats, and they have their moments, but there's always a feeling that they could turn their back on you at any moment for any reason or none at all and be perfectly happy. Luna hammered that into me.

Dogs don't do that.

The clincher, the final straw that lit my insistence into obsession? I found a book in the back of Cass's barn that summer, a really, *really* old book. It was called "Lad: A Dog," and Cass and I nearly fought over it, since it was her barn, but I agreed to share. I'm sure you've never heard of it, because it was published, believe it or not, in 1919! The copy I found was almost that old, and kinda beat up, but I took it home and read it, surprising everyone.

Then I read it again.

Oh.

My.

God.

I wanted a collie. I wanted *Lad*, a loyal, loving, clever, playful, smart dog. I'd been talking about it, non-stop, since I finished the book. My folks, Cass, her folks, the kids at school, the teachers, and strangers when we went shopping. I'd even cornered Shawn and talked to him until he ran away and I had to tackle him to finish my sentence.

Yeah. Maybe I was a little obsessive. Perhaps. Not so you'd notice, right?

Mama and Dad used to have pets, but from the time I was old enough to ask for one their answer was always the same: once I could take care of it, they'd consider it. Well, I was seven now. I could take care of a dog!

Anyways, it was the only thing I could think of, so I said, "Um. Maybe. Can I?"

"Kendra Marissa, you know the rules." It was never a good sign when he used my middle name, but I wasn't giving up. Not with a puppy in play!

I tried my best legalese on him. I'd been listening to him all my life, after all, and I'd picked up a few tricks. "Dad, you brought it up. If you didn't intend to let me amind the list, you shouldn't have said anything. You did, eggo you meant to give me a chance."

By the time I finished my little speech Dad was smiling.

"Your logic is sound, Kendra. Yes, I intend to let you *amend* the list, just this once, and only a single item. You understand that this is a one-time exception?"

My neck was getting sore from bobbing my head up and down as he spoke. "I understand, I understand, I understand!"

He grandly handed the list back to me.

"Very well. Make your addition."

I tried not to run with it; I think I managed a fast walk. I was furiously considering how to word it. I couldn't just write,

"Puppy," because while I'd get a puppy, sure, it wouldn't be the right one. I had to be specific, but I couldn't be wordy because, well, I hadn't left much room on the paper.

This is what I wrote:

Collie puppy, male, rough sable, champion parentage with a broad head and soulful eyes.

Was it a tall order? Maybe. But I knew what I wanted, Lad, and that's how he was described in the book.

I wrote it most carefully. I knew my handwriting could get sloppy if I rushed, and this was too important for me to screw up. I marched back to Dad and held out the updated list.

He hesitated, with his hand hovering over it, and said, "You're sure? You have it exactly how you want it?"

I pulled it back and looked again.

"Yes," and I put it in his hand. He folded it without even a glance and nodded once. "I'll see what we can do."

In a flash I was out of the room and down the hall to the room we were sharing. The door was closed but I didn't stop to knock.

"I'm getting a puppy!" I yelled once I was inside. I heard a *clunk!,* then an "Ow!"

That didn't make any sense as a response, so I added, "Did you hear me? What?"

She rubbed her head. That's when I noticed she'd been bent over, doing something with her tools, and...

Oops.

"Sorry," I said, stepping more sedately, careful not to crush anything on the floor. I looked at her head, where her hand was. We learned a basic knowledge of first aid early. "You're not bleeding."

She removed her hand and peered at it, to verify my statement, I guess. "What did you say? A puppy?"

"Uh-huh!"

"Your parents are getting you a puppy?"

"Uh-huh!"

Her head tilted. "How are you so sure?"

"It's on my Christmas list!"

She looked at me with a mixture of tolerance and understanding which I've seen from her all my life, and still do. With infinite patience, she said, "Kendra, you've been putting puppy or kitten or hamster on your list every year and haven't gotten any yet."

"But this year is different!" I insisted.

"And that's what you said last year."

"But it *is*!"

"How?"

I explained. By the time I finished her expression had changed from doubt to possibility.

"I'll believe it when I see it," she said. "But maybe you're right."

I hugged her. Cass saying I was right was almost as good as reading it in a book, and better than the word of a god.

"Hey, let go!"

I dropped her, having not realized I'd lifted her from the floor. "I know what I'm going to name him, too!"

"Lad?"

"How'd you guess?"

She rolled her eyes.

"It's all you've talked about since summer, Kendra."

"Oh, yeah. But Cass, a puppy! This is going to be so much fun! You'll help, right? Because I don't know anything about raising puppies." I looked at her and played my trump card. "You learned how to be a big sister, so how hard can a puppy be?"

"Being a big sister is hard, but we'll figure your puppy out."

A puppy!

Christmas Surprises

YOU KNOW WHAT IT'S like when time doesn't seem to move?

I do.

From the day I gave Dad my list, time slowed down. The closer we got to the day of the party, the slower it went.

Christmas crawled past.

What? My puppy? Oh, no, I didn't get it on Christmas day.

See, we always celebrated with the Cassidy's. Some years we'd host, some years they'd host. Tammie didn't celebrate Christmas, she celebrated the Solstice, and Charles more or less went along with what she did. Christmas Day, then, wasn't a big deal in Cass's home. In deference to Tammie's beliefs, we tried to avoid doing the gathering on the day. Dad was a politician, after all, and knew the value of not offending people even unintentionally.

In '87, Christmas was on a Thursday, so the party was planned for Friday.

But I'm getting head of myself. I was talking about the month between the list and the party.

At first, it was just me feeling it. I was bubbling, okay? I couldn't help myself. My dreams were all about that puppy, and I was never good at waiting. So I talked about it, and talked about it, and talked about it.

Him, I should say. I mean, I asked for a boy puppy, and so I was gonna *get* a boy puppy. That's how it worked. Either I got what was on the list, exactly as it was on the list, or I didn't. There wasn't an almost or just about. All or nothing was Dad's way, and I learned from him. Nobody anyone who knows me now would be surprised, as that's how I roll. Drives Cass nuts now, like it did then, but I can't help it.

But I was all in on this puppy.

Once Cass was convinced, she became her usual helpful self. She found all sorts of things for me to read and watch, hoping I'd learn how to raise a puppy.

"This tells me everything I need," I said, waving "Lad" at her. I'd let her borrow it and was picking it up from her, maybe a few days into December. "Remember when Lad was raising Wolf?"

She shook her head. "You're not a dog."

"Hey!"

"I mean it in a good way, knucklehead." She smiled at me and my annoyance melted. This is also something she can still do. "If the writer had told you how he raised Lad, that would be different, because he sounds like he was the perfect dog. But he doesn't, or at least not in that book."

I latched onto the last words. "He did somewhere else?"

Cass seemed to recognize her error, but rallied. "Well, not really, but he talked about raising other dogs who ended up on Sunnybank, and I think you can start there."

I was psyched. I liked to read, sometimes, when the subject interested me. I hoped for another antique book, but was disappointed.

"I sent them to your padd."

"Them? Padd? Ebooks?" My enthusiasm fell a bit. I preferred holding books in my hands instead of reading them on a screen, but I could deal. This was for the puppy.

"A bunch. Yep. Your Mama helped. I also sent you some more modern books and stuff on raising puppies."

This sounded like homework. "Oh boy. More reading."

My tone must've given me away, because Cass said, "It's not all reading! There's lots of fun videos."

"Fun? Says who?"

"Well…"

I took a breath before I said anything else. I knew Cass was trying to help. Just because she was reading books from my Mama's library didn't mean what she found wouldn't be good. "Thank you. I'll watch them. Will you watch with me?"

"Oh, sure!" she said, then her tone brightened. "And we have to find toys."

"Toys?" I was a little confused. I had plenty of toys, and Kaeli was still too little to appreciate them.

"For the puppy."

"Right!" Of course. Not toys for me or her sister.

"And a bed."

"I want him to sleep with me."

Cass waggled her hand. "Maybe after he's housebroken."

"Huh?"

She sighed. "Housebroken. Not going potty in the house."

"Oh." Another detail I hadn't considered.

"And then there's…"

She went on for a while, and I started to understand the enormity of my undertaking. But with Cass helping me, I was sure I'd understand, so I dove in.

Pretty soon both families were caught up in the impending puppypocalypse, and I couldn't help but be cheered by it. I explained my thoughts to Cass one night after bed, in whispers since it was a school night and we were supposed to be sleeping.

"If I wasn't getting a puppy, Mama and Dad wouldn't have brought us to Grand Forks to pick up all that stuff, right?" I said for the fourth or fifth time.

"Makes sense," she agreed, then yawned. "Kendra, can we *please* go to sleep now?"

"But it's next week!"

"And it will get here quicker if you sleep!" I knew she was clever, and this proved it. If anything would shut me up, time moving faster was it.

I almost managed to put the puppy out of my mind that weekend. It was the Solstice, and so Cass and I were kept busy by Tammie, helping her prepare. More accurately, Cass helped prepare, and my purpose was shadowing Shawn to prevent a recurrence of the prior year's disaster.

He hated it, and me, but I hated him most of the time, so we were even.

To do my job, I got to spend the entire weekend with them, from Thursday night onward. I loved it. Kaeli was almost sleeping through the night, so our extended sleepover would be ending soon. Spending time with Cass in her home was an unexpected bonus.

Cass helped me out, too. She hacked into her family security system so I could track him when I had to be elsewhere. Between this tweak and my devotion to my job? There weren't any fireworks in the bonfire that Solstice.

He never even thanked me for keeping him out of trouble. Ungrateful!

But then it was finally the week, and I swear to you, time stopped. I think it was Monday for about a year. Tuesday took at least a decade to pass. Wednesday? Easily a century. Thursday was Christmas, and you know how it never seems to last when you're a kid?

How about a Christmas that never ends?

Let me tell you, it's objectively terrible.

I loved all the winter holidays; I still do. Christmas, Solstice, Hanukkah, Kwanzaa, doesn't matter. It's a reason to reunite with family, and that's enough for me. The only problem is the gatherings end too soon, as commitments call people away.

But that Christmas? I couldn't wait for it to end.

Finally, *finally*, it was time for bed, and I nearly jumped under the covers. Cass, who'd come back to my house after the Solistice weekend, groaned.

"I won't wriggle!"

She grunted.

"I won't, promise! I'm gonna go right to sleep."

Cass rolled over, facing away from me, and buried her head under a pillow. Dramatic, but it worked, and she was asleep in minutes.

I was ready to follow her. The sooner I slept, the quicker morning would come.

Right.

I could do this.

Nope. I couldn't sleep.

I lay there thinking, *Sleep. Sleep. I just have to go to sleep. If I go to sleep then when I wake up it'll be tomorrow. And I'll have my puppy. But I can't sleep. I have to sleep. Sleep!*

Which is entirely the wrong thing to try to think when you're trying to sleep.

Eventually I fell asleep, of course, and I don't think I woke up more than six or seven times overnight, going through the whole routine again.

Finally it was morning, and I bounced out of bed...

No, not really.

Mama came in and gently shook me awake.

"Morning, sleepyhead," she said. I opened an eye and blearily looked at her. Cass was already up, I noticed, her side of the bed empty.

"Morning Mama," I mumbled and closed my eye. "Wanna sleep more."

"You do?" Her tone was gentle.

"Uh-huh."

"You're sure?"

"Uh-huh. Tired."

"Tired. Gee, sweetie, why are you tired?"

Why was she asking me all these questions? It wasn't a school day, it was vacation, I could sleep if I wanted. "Din't sleep much."

"I see. Why?"

Despite my sleep-fuzzed brain, something about her persistence penetrated. "Huh?"

"Do you remember why you didn't sleep much?"

I forced my brain to make connections no matter how it objected. Finally the thought surfaced.

"Excited about opening my presents – *my puppy!*"

I was out of bed and running for the bedroom door before my eyes opened fully.

"Wait, wait, wait!"

I grabbed the frame and skidded to a halt. "What?"

"We're not opening presents yet."

"Mama!" I wailed. Yes, I wailed. It was like falling down two meters short of the finish line after running a marathon.

She continued, completely ignoring me. "We're going out with Aiyana and her family. She's already up and back home to change. Since you slept so late, you barely have time for a shower and breakfast before they get here."

"I don't need a shower, it's just Cass!" Mama always called her Aiyana, the lone holdout to the universality of her nickname.

"You do. We're going out, or did you miss me saying it?" When Mama got sarcastic I knew I'd better back off.

"No, Mama."

"Very well. I'll expect you for breakfast in fifteen minutes. Your father is making waffles."

Waffles. Sure-fire motivation. "From scratch?"

"Since when does he do anything else? From scratch."

Okay. I could deal with the delay for waffles.

"And make sure you use soap!"

Twelve minutes later, more or less showered and dressed in the outfit Mama laid out for me, I was sitting at the breakfast table. I thought the dress she had me wearing was a little fancy for opening presents, but I didn't know why we were going out.

Besides, *Mama*. I'd learned she had a whim of iron. Crossing it wasn't a good idea, but I could ask questions if I didn't understand.

"Mama, why did you choose this dress for me today?" That was safe enough, questioning the specific dress and not the entire dress-wearing thing. Or her picking out my clothes, which she hadn't done since I was little-little.

"Because we're going out and it's important you look nice."

Okay, a non-answer for a non-question. Dad filled in the silence as we waited for the waffle to finish.

"Kendra, today's an important day. Do you know why?"

If it wasn't because I was getting my puppy, I didn't much care. "Because I'm getting my puppy?"

He and Mama exchanged a look. "Sort of," he said. "You are getting your puppy today, and, oof!"

I'd teleported over to him and wrapped him in a hug. "Thank you!" I gibbered, over and over.

"You're welcome," he said, trying for paternal. "Now, sit down and I'll explain."

He checked on the waffle in the iron as I sat again.

"We're not buying your dog, Kendra." Before my shocked look converted to a protest, he continued. "Well, no. We are, but it's more than giving them money and getting a dog. We're adopting him. Do you know what the difference is?"

"No." I didn't think this was fair, giving me questions and new ideas before breakfast.

"Anyone can buy a dog, from someone who doesn't care where the puppies end up. They might end up in a good home or a bad one, and as long as the seller gets the money, they don't care. Adoption is more serious. To be adopted means that the family where the dog came from thinks the family the dog goes to is a good fit, loving and kind. They'll take care of the dog, give him a safe place to grow and learn and become the best dog he can be. Does that make sense?"

As he spoke he got the waffle out and put it on a plate in front of me, but didn't slide it over until I looked at him. I forced my brain to process what he said, not the steaming pastry, and definitely not my growling stomach. "I think so, Dad. It's special, right?"

"Very special, punkin," he agreed, and I got the plate. "Syrup or strawberries?"

"Can I have two waffles?"

"When do you not?" He knew me so well.

"Then strawberries to begin, please."

There was no talking while I ate, and it gave me a chance to think about what Dad said. It made sense, the more I considered it. I certainly wouldn't want a puppy to come from someone who didn't care where it went. And if I ever was in a place where I had puppies to send out, I'd want to know they were going to people who'd treat them right. Only one thing confused me, and when I finished the first waffle I asked.

"Dad, why does Cass have to come?"

His eyes flicked to Mama, but he didn't hesitate. "It's an important day for you, and I thought you'd want your best friend with you."

Fair enough. I dug into the second waffle.

Cass and her family arrived while I was mopping up the last drops of syrup. She'd gone home to dress nicely because she wasn't in her usual jeans and shirt. That just reinforced how special this was.

"We're going to get my puppy!" I announced as soon as she walked into the kitchen.

"I know. Mom said we get to come because it's a special day."

I nodded. "An adoption."

Cass slid onto the stool beside me. "Is there another, thank you, Mr. Briggs," she said, as Dad put a plated waffle in front of her with butter and syrup.

"I thought you might be hungry. Kendra?"

I pondered the unspoken question carefully. This was a weighty matter, after all. To waffle, or not to waffle?

"Half?"

"If Cass will eat the other half."

She nodded, her mouth busy.

"Okay, a half for each of you."

I didn't notice Mama slip out of the kitchen with Tammie and Charles, but as we were finishing our halves I saw them come back.

"Ready to go?" she asked. "We don't want to be late."

"Ready!" I said around my last mouthful.

"Kendra, no talking around your food."

I chewed and nodded, taking my plate and putting it in the dishwasher.

"Ready!" agreed Cass, copying me.

We all piled into the new, bigger car Dad had gotten in the summer, when it became clear we were going to be doing more things with Cass and her family and so needed a way to travel together. Cass and I piled into the back, as usual, and started talking.

After about twenty minutes I looked around and realized I knew where we were: Crookston.

"Dad? Is this where the puppy is?"

"No, but we have to make a stop first." We were pulling in front of the courthouse as he said it.

"Why?" I didn't whine much, I promise.

"It's important, Kendra, and shouldn't take long. We have to do this before we get the dog."

Ah. An adulting thing. Okay, I knew they existed. Didn't understand them, and found them awfully inconvenient, but whatever. As long as my puppy was at the end of the line, I was game.

Mama and Dad got out, followed by Cass's folks and siblings. Cass and I followed, not wanting to stay in the stopped car in the cold. We went up to the door but, to my surprise, had to wait for it to be opened from inside. That never happened before. Dad nodded to the uniformed guard as he passed.

He must have sensed my question because he said, "I made special arrangements to do this, they're supposed to be closed for the holiday weekend but the Judge is a friend of mine."

Judge?

We walked down the silent corridors. I'd been here a few times, checking in with my case worker. We weren't going to see them, though. How did I know? Their office was in the basement of the courthouse, but we weren't going to the basement, and anyway, Ms. Aquilera wasn't a Judge.

Dad stopped at a huge, ornate wooden door, dark and imposing.

"Kendra." His voice was terribly serious, and I was suddenly worried.

"Yes, Dad?"

"The Judge might ask you some questions. If he does, answer them honestly, no matter what. Understand me?" Was that a hint of nerves? In Dad's voice?

"I do, sort of, but why will he ask questions? Am I in trouble?" I don't know why I leapt to that. I hadn't done anything which would warrant adult attention, much less a judge, in weeks and weeks. For me this was nearly unprecedented.

"No, you're not in trouble." There was something more he wanted to say, but I couldn't figure it out and he was having a hard time too. Finally he said, "If he asks anything, it will be about home and what you like."

"Um. Like my room and things like that?" I tried to wrap my mind about why a Judge would care about my room and failed.

"Anything, sweetie. And remember this: no matter what happens, your mother and I love you very much."

Cancel worried. Make that scared.

"Dad?"

He heard the quaver and wrapped me up in a hug. "It will be fine. It'll all work out the way it's supposed to."

With that he released me but held onto my hand. Mama took my other hand, and together we marched into the courtroom.

I'd never been in one before, and I'll admit I spent much of my time looking around and gawking. The walls were all dark wood, with row upon row of benches leading up to the front. The Judge sat in the front, way up high behind a massive bench, looking both proper and out of place. He was wearing a plaid shirt and smiling. Smiling? Judges weren't supposed to smile. At least, none of the Judges I'd ever seen on video smiled. Well, except that one, but he was supposed to be funny. I didn't know much about real courts, but I'd watched shows which showed them and while I could figure out they weren't really real I kinda assumed they had some basis in fact. This smiling, kindly-looking, white-haired guy in a comfortable shirt didn't match anything I knew.

I noticed another detail.

"Isn't he supposed to be in a robe?"

"It's officially a day off. Like I said, he's doing this as a favor." He pitched his voice to carry. "Good morning, Harry. Thanks for this."

"It's easy enough," he answered in a deep, deep voice which put me in mind of warm, fuzzy blankets. "Is this the young lady?"

We were down before his bench now, and I leaned back to look up.

"Yes. Judge Harry Stone, this is Kendra. Kendra Marissa Smith." He nudged me.

"Hello, Judge Stone."

"Miss Smith." He picked up a folder on his desk and riffed through the pages. "Relax. You're not in trouble. I'm just going to ask a few questions."

His smile reassured me. Surely this wasn't anything bad.

"According to this, you've been living with Dr. Foster and Mr. Briggs for over seven years."

It sounded right to me and I said so.

"And do you like it there?"

"Yes, Judge Stone, I do." Mama gave my hand a little squeeze.

"What do you like about it? It can be anything."

"Well, I like my room," I began. I sensed this wasn't quite what he was looking for and elaborated. "I get waffles, though not all the time. Mama says they're not good for me to have every day."

"By Mama, you mean Dr. Foster?"

I looked up and saw her smile. "Yes."

"Did she ask you to call her that?"

"No, Judge."

"Then why do you call her Mama?"

"Because she is, Judge, she's my mama." How do you explain to a stranger why your mother is your mother? I didn't know then, and I don't know now.

"And what do you call Mr. Briggs?"

I turned. "You mean Dad?"

"That answers my question. Are you happy, Miss Smith, living with, ah, Mama and Dad?"

"I can't imagine living anywhere else. Well, except maybe with Cass and her family. But I kinda sorta do, at least as much as she lives with us, too." I think I confused him.

"Who is Cass, Miss Smith?"

Cass came up and hugged me from behind, catching the judge's eye.

"Introduce yourself, please," he said. Cass released me and stood up straight, showing her height.

"Aiyana Cassidy, Your Honor."

Oh, yeah. That was the other way to address a judge.

"And what is your relationship to Miss Smith?"

"I love her, Your Honor. She's my best friend. We do everything together."

"Everything?"

"She's my sister, Your Honor, in every way that counts."

"Hmm. Is that accurate, Miss Smith?"

"It is, Your Honor. I love her, too."

Dad interrupted. "If I may explain?"

"Go ahead."

"The Cassidy's are our neighbors, and Cass – Aiyana – was born a few weeks before Kendra. They've essentially grown up together, and have forged a bond as close as any blood siblings."

"Closer," Cass whispered, and I giggled. She must have meant Shawn. The judge gave me a stern look but didn't say anything to me.

"They certainly appear close," he said instead. "Very well. Miss Smith, one more question."

I nodded.

"Imagine you could live anywhere in the world, with anyone you wanted. What does that look like?"

My answer was instantaneous.

"Right where I am. I don't want to leave, not Mama, not Dad, not Cass, not even Shawn!" I heard his surprised grunt from far behind. "I mean, maybe I'd like to live somewhere warmer, but only if they can all be there, too!"

That drew a smile back to his face. "Very well. I've heard enough. Official record begin."

A robotic voice said, "Recording."

"In the matter of Imperium vs. Jane Foster and Harold Briggs, regarding the custody of the minor child Kendra

Marissa Smith, this court finds in favor of Foster and Briggs. Furthermore, in the matter of Jane Foster and Harold Briggs, Adoption Case 87 dash 413, this court will issue a Final Decree of Adoption on this date, 26 December 2087, in favor of the Plaintiffs. Further, this court waives the consent of the biological mother, Jane Doe 32, currently in the care of the government of Big Sky, and the biological father, unknown. End record."

I found myself pressed between my parents who were simultaneously crying and laughing and trying to squeeze the air out of me. There were more tears as they thanked the judge.

"One moment," he said, as we tried to leave. I'd had enough and thought I was doing particularly well at being patient.

"Miss Smith."

"Judge?" Whatever he wanted, I hoped it would be quick. I had a puppy to get.

"When a child is adopted, their name is often changed to reflect their new family. Would you like to do so? What you answer isn't legally binding, but rather a guide for your parents."

"I like Kendra," I said, not quite grasping the question.

"Your last name. Smith."

"Oh." I was still catching up on everything. "Um. Can I have both names?"

He seemed confused. "You wish to keep Smith and add another name?"

"No, Mama and Dad. Foster and Briggs."

"Foster-Briggs? Kendra Foster-Briggs?"

I didn't answer immediately, taking a moment to think for once, rolling it over in my mind. It felt good.

"Yes."

"Dr. Foster? Hal? Any objections?"

Apparently my announcement had caused another attack of the weepies because they didn't say anything. I could feel their headshakes, though, and I guess that was enough for the Judge.

"I'll enter that as well and have a certified copy to send with the rest of the order. Kendra, I hope you realize how lucky you are to have such wonderful people as your parents, whether you share any blood or not."

I didn't know what he meant, but I thought they were pretty cool. After all, they were the only parents I'd ever known. I agreed.

"Then I won't keep you any longer." We left hastily, and I was pretty proud of myself for not mentioning anything about my puppy until we were out of the building.

"Now can we pick up my puppy?"

All the adults laughed. "Yes, we'll go get your puppy," Mama said.

A little while later I noticed Cass staring at me, her eyes wide. "What?"

"Do you know what just happened, Kendra?"

"I got to change my name and get asked some silly questions."

"Kendra, you've been *adopted!*"

I still didn't get it.

"It means that your Mama and Dad are your forever home, now."

"They always were. Why are you shaking your head?"

"Because they *weren't*. They were your foster parents."

"I know that."

"That means they were looking after you because your real mother, the woman who gave birth to you, and your birth father can't or won't."

This I sort of knew. I knew that Mama didn't carry me, that another woman did. I even remembered one trip we'd taken when I was younger, to the hospital in Big Sky, and I'd gotten a chance to see the pale, waxy figure in the bed, hooked up to all the machines keeping her alive. It had upset me enough we'd never been back.

"Okay...so?"

Cass huffed in impatience. "Before today, if your mother woke up and said she wanted you to live with her, you'd have to go."

"No!" I was probably a little loud, but I didn't care. Leave Mama and Dad for some stranger? Someone I didn't know?

"*Before* today," Cass emphasized. "Now, she can't. Nobody can. That's what I mean by forever home, Kendra!"

"I've been...adopted." It was starting to sink in. "Like I'm adopting the puppy."

"Not quite," Tammie said, turning around and injecting herself into our conversation. "Your parents have been working on this for many years, Kendra, since you were about two."

"Why'd it take 'til now?"

"From what I've been told, it was the Imperium. They're reluctant to terminate parental rights too quickly, but you've been with Jane and Hal for seven years now. That was the only objection the Imperium could muster, so what Judge Stone did today was the final step."

"Five years they've wanted to do this?"

Tammie nodded. "They love you very much, Kendra."

Now I was getting the weepies as the magnitude of what they'd done started to sink in.

"Forever and ever?" I said in a small voice.

"Forever and ever," agreed Tammie. "And you'll be part of our family just as long."

Cass emphasized the point by hugging me tight.

"I meant what I said, Kendra. You're the best sister I've ever had."

"And the other part, too?"

She giggled. "Of course, silly."

Adopted. I was *adopted*.

I had a family. Better, I had Cass. And I was getting a puppy.

Best.

Christmas.

Ever.

Finally, a Puppy!

YOU WOULD THINK, AFTER the excitement of the morning, that nothing could top it. Ha.

The family who had Lad lived in Red Lake Falls, the seat of the next county over and about forty kilometers away. For the first part of the ride, I was quiet. Happy, yes, but the enormity of what happened was still sinking in.

I pressed my face against the car window, watching the world whiz by in a blur of green fields and blue sky. Cass sat next to me, bouncing with energy as she chattered on about all the fun adventures she imagined Lad and I would have together.

"Kendra, do you think Lad will like me?" Aiyana asked, her eyes wide with anticipation.

I nodded eagerly. "Of course he will! You're the best, Cass."

Mama glanced back at us from the front seat, a smile playing at the corners of her lips. "You two are going to be the best of friends."

Dad hummed along to the radio, his fingers tapping against the steering wheel in time with the music. He glanced at Mom and gave her a wink. "I can't believe we're getting a puppy."

Mama chuckled. "It's about time. Kendra's been asking for one since she could talk."

I grinned, feeling a surge of excitement bubble up inside me. Today was the day we were bringing Lad home, the newest addition to our family. The morning's events replayed in my mind, a cherished memory, reminding me of the journey that led me to this moment.

Just a few hours ago, I stood in an empty courtroom, my heart pounding with nervous anticipation. It was the day my parents officially adopted me, welcoming me into their lives with open arms and overflowing love. As I looked around the room at the familiar faces of my family, I felt a sense of belonging wash over me, knowing that I was finally home.

And now, as we prepared to bring Lad home, I couldn't help but notice the parallels between my adoption and what we were doing for him. Just like my parents had chosen me to be a part of their family, we had chosen Lad to be a part of ours. It was a powerful realization, filling me with a profound sense of gratitude and joy.

As we pulled into the driveway of the farmhouse where Lad was waiting for us, my heart raced with anticipation. The air was thick with the scent of snow, and the clouds loomed low, but I didn't care. I practically leaped out of the car, eager to greet Lad.

Mama and Dad exchanged a knowing glance before they caught up to me, gently reminding me to be calm. "Remember, Kendra, Lad is just a little puppy," Mama said, her voice soft but firm. "He might be excited too, so we all have to behave."

Dad nodded in agreement. "That's right. We need to give Lad time to adjust to his new family, and his new home."

I nodded, trying to contain my excitement as we approached the farmhouse. The seller, a kind-hearted woman with a warm smile, greeted us at the door. She welcomed us inside, leading us to a cozy room where Lad's mother and siblings were waiting.

The sight of the other puppies, cuddled up together with their mother, filled me with a sense of warmth and comfort. I watched in awe as Lad's mother nuzzled her pups, her gentle eyes filled with love and affection.

And then I saw him – Lad. He was smaller than I expected, with soft fur and big, curious eyes that seemed to sparkle with mischief. I felt an instant connection with him, as if we had known each other forever. He was a vision of pure delight as I gazed upon him. His fluffy coat, a medley of creamy whites, rich browns, and deep blacks, enveloped him like a soft blanket, inviting me to run my fingers through its silky strands. Each touch revealed the warmth of his affection, as if his fur held the secrets of boundless love within its soft embrace.

His eyes, bright and expressive, sparkled with intelligence and kindness, reflecting the gentle nature that seemed to radiate from his very being. They seemed to hold a depth of understanding far beyond his youthful innocence, drawing me in with their silent invitation to share in his world.

With every graceful movement, Lad exuded an air of elegance and poise that belied his tender age. His slender frame hinted at the athleticism that would surely blossom as he grew, promising a future filled with agility and strength.

His ears added to his endearing appearance, giving him a look of perpetual alertness and attentiveness. It was as if he was always ready to listen, to learn, to explore the wonders of the world around him.

But amidst his regal demeanor, Lad's playful spirit shone through with undeniable vigor. He bounded around with boundless energy, his wagging tail and joyful barks a testament to his exuberance and zest for life. Watching him chase after toys and explore his new surroundings filled me with a sense of joy and wonder, as if I was witnessing the pure essence of happiness in motion.

Above all, Lad exuded warmth and affection, eager to shower his family with love and loyalty. It was as if he knew he was destined to become an integral part of our lives, his gentle nature and unwavering devotion already capturing the hearts of all who were lucky enough to welcome him into our home.

Lad spotted me too, his tail wagging eagerly as he bounded over to greet me. With a playful bark, he sat down in front of me and offered his paw in greeting. I laughed with delight, feeling a rush of happiness wash over me.

"He likes you, Kendra," Aiyana said, her eyes shining with excitement. "You're going to be the best of friends."

I tore my eyes from Lad to look right into hers. "No, you're my best friend. But he's gonna be the *best* dog!"

Memories of Aiyana: After

WELL, OF COURSE THERE'S an after.

But not now.

I'll be back in a while with more stories from our childhood. Our lives got crazier and crazier for the next few years, despite living in the end of nowhere.

If you want to reach me, you can send me an email to kendra.m.cassidy@gmail.com.

Don't ask me how Adam set these things up to reach me in the *when* I'm at these days, because I don't know. But they get through!

And if you want to keep up with Adam and the ~~nonsense~~ stories he's writing about us and my Terran Federation, check out his website, https://cassidychronicles.com.

Until next time!

Kendra Cassidy

Admiral, Terran Federation (Ret.)

Editor's Afterword

(2025 UPDATE: WE WON! BEST Middle Grade Novel – this is across ALL genres – at the Imaginarium Convention! It's the Imadjinn 2025 WINNER!)

Editing for Kendra is a trip.

Do you know how Mac speaks? Well, don't tell Kendra, but that's what she does, too. Not quite as stream-of-consciousness, maybe, and a hair slower, but she can leap from subject to subject as easily as a cat leaps after a dog.

Yes, I know what I wrote there.

If you ever meet me, you'll know why.

She and I went round and round over this book. It's not that she tells stories badly; quite the contrary! She's an enthusiastic and fun storyteller with a natural gift for pacing. I loved hearing her tell the stories, returning to her childhood. Her fondness for the flea speck which will be Key West is evident in her voice when she speaks of it.

The problem was a) keeping her on track and b) keeping the details down.

My god, the woman has a memory that an AI would be proud of!

I'll tell you a little secret: the places in here where she's being vague about a detail? That's me. If I hadn't, well, this book would be about double the length and cover half the time span.

Seriously.

And I can't wait to do the next one.

And now for *my* thank-yous!

Let's begin with my Beta readers. – Crystal, Tim, Jim, Jim, Drew, Rebecca, and Lauren. I love the enthusiasm I always get when I ask for early readers, even though you know the cake is only half-baked!

I also want to thank my Patrons. George, Letty, Adam, Ben, Jim, and Rita.

My wife, who not only had to put up with her author husband but this blonde telling outrageous stories. Fortunately (or maybe worryingly) they got along swimmingly. Thank you for loving me.

And of course, you. Thank you for reading what I put out there and coming back for more. Keep up with me at https://adamgaffenauthor.com.

Adam

'Writing is antisocial. It's as solitary as masturbation. Disturb a writer when he is in the throes of creation and he is likely to turn and bite right to the bone... and not even know that he's doing it. As writers' wives and husbands often learn to their horror...There is no way that writers can be tamed and rendered civilized. Or even cured. In a household with more than one person, of which one is a writer, the only solution known to science is to provide the patient with an isolation room, where he can endure the acute stages in private, and where food can be poked in to him with a stick. Because, if you disturb the patient at such times, he may break into tears or become violent. Or he may not hear you at all... and, if you shake him at this stage, he bites...' – Robert A. Heinlein

Don't leave yet!
Keep reading for a story based on the "Helloween" chapter
AND
The story of Kendra and Aiyana's first kiss – previously available as the stories "Magic for Skeptics" and "Kendra and the Fae" – is now available to YOU as an exclusive free bonus for buyers of this book!
Just follow this link and you can download "A Christmas Kiss"
https://dl.bookfunnel.com/8v0yd5k62w

Helloween: A Shakespearean Tale

[I THOUGHT YOU MIGHT enjoy a version of the Helloween chapter, written as if the Bard wrote it. Okay, it's not for you; this one's for my love, since she's had a crush on Shakespeare since we were kids and she's been truly patient with me for more years than I want to count.]

Hark! Attend thee closely to my tale, a curious yarn of youthful revelry and masquerade. 'Twas not a mistake or misdeed, but a whimsical season known as Helloween, where mirth and guises held sway.

In garments of yore, we robed ourselves, forsooth! From our elders' raiments, attires of bygone kin, a hoarder's bounty did furnish our attires. A diplomat's dwelling, a treasure trove it became, for in distant realms he trod, collecting wares and artworks aplenty.

This diplomat, a prosperous soul, called out for consultation, his merits echoing though retired he be for three winters past. Lost in my musings, verily, my discourse did stray. Clothes! Inherited vestments, a motley array, bestowed upon my person, a wardrobe of antiquity.

Methinks, could my fondness for the early 21st Century stem from my father's trinkets? A notion pondered as Aiyana, too, did delve into my apparel trove, partaking liberally of its eclectic fare.

In the month of October, Helloween's advent approached. A time for mirthful escapades, where fanciful characters we'd become, parading in our masquerade. Policemen, teachers, farmers – mundane roles intermingled with the fantastical.

We, daring souls, embarked on a sartorial adventure. Politician, soldier, diplomat – the gamut of personas unfolded. Deeper still, rebels from a bygone war we became. A creative spark ignited as Mama granted leave to alter garments, transforming them into a canvas for our ingenuity.

A Thursday arrived, and Cass and I, in veils and filmy skirts, assumed the guise of bellydancers. Mystified by the allure, other children sought to emulate our undulations.

Yet, Halloween beckoned, and aspirations soared higher. By '86, enthralled by televised fables, Buffy the Vampire Slayer enthused our spirits. Thus, Willow and Buffy became our envisioned identities. Teenager clothes, simple props, and emulation of characters – we endeavored, mastering the choreography from the screened sagas.

The challenges ascended in mastering martial arts, a pursuit relentless as we rehearsed and mimicked our celluloid inspirations. A week prior to Hallow's eve, our commitment manifested – as Buffy and Willow, we'd stride through daylight, our parents obliged to address us by these fictional monikers.

Alas, Cass, draped as Willow, perhaps enjoyed a solace in her modest attire compared to my Buffy's scant raiment, a plight in chilly October.

Astride the school bus, the decree to name us Buffy and Willow echoed. By the eve's end, our nomenclature pervaded the school, from pupils to teachers, a collective transformation.

Hallow's eve approached, and a theatrical tapestry unfolded. Vampires, werewolves, and creatures nocturnal graced the halls of our modest school. Teachers embraced roles as principal, librarian, and technomancer.

On a fateful Tuesday, a mock vampire surfaced, heralding a cascade of fanciful adversaries by week's end. The school, reshaped into Sunnydale, embraced the revelry, donning guises to emulate characters.

Yet, the winds of Wednesday brought an unexpected twist. Recess transpired, only to conclude with Cass missing. Distressed, inquiries ensued, and a mysterious note, inscribed by a 6-year-old hand, portended dire tidings – "Send Buffy or Willow dies – the Master."

In disbelief, I traversed the halls, ensnared by unseen hands, a bag over my visage. Minutes later, the veil lifted, revealing a gym supply closet. "Kendra!" echoed, and there stood Cass, captive in the clutches of discontented children.

A proclamation resounded, foretelling doom as retribution for my supposed transgressions. Cass screamed, and a visceral rage overcame me. A ballet of kicks and punches ensued, propelled by the echoes of practiced moves from televised tales.

A harrowing interlude transpired, culminating in the revelation of the Master's design. Chaos and bloodshed painted the canvas, the stakes no longer mere props. As the dust settled, the tale's denouement unfolded.

Lyssa's wounded arm, the writhing Jeremy, and the stake-wielding protagonist – a tableau etched in memory. The principal sought to discern the narrative, and Cass, once calmed, articulated our innocence.

The note, a vindication etched by youthful hands, became my shield. Justified in my actions, the masquerade had not transgressed into malevolence. An accord reached, no repercussions befell, yet the days of costume-wearing were curtailed.

Curiously, Lyssa and I forged an amicable friendship. The bitterness uncoiled, replaced by camaraderie. A curious chapter, enigmatic and whimsical, concluded, paving the way for subsequent escapades in the annals of the Federation.

Don't miss out!

Visit the website below and you can sign up to receive emails whenever Adam Gaffen publishes a new book. There's no charge and no obligation.

https://books2read.com/r/B-A-PBTN-OWXZC

BOOKS 2 READ

Connecting independent readers to independent writers.

Did you love *Quantum Quirks: A Science Fiction Childhood*? Then you should read *The Cassidy Chronicles - The Spark Before the Fire*[1] by Adam Gaffen!

Her wedding ended in gunfire. Now she's running for her life—and fighting for a future worth building.

Aiyana Cassidy wanted one perfect day.

She had the partner of her dreams. A quiet ceremony. A life of science, invention, and possibility ahead of her. But when the minister pulled a gun, everything changed.

Now she and her wife Kendra are on the run across a divided America—a patchwork of independent nations and

---

1. https://books2read.com/u/bpz0qW

2. https://books2read.com/u/bpz0qW

power-hungry factions where freedom is relative and safety is a luxury. They don't know who wants them dead, or why. All they know is that it started at the altar, and it hasn't stopped since.

Kendra Cassidy is nobody's damsel. Raised in shadows and trained for survival, she knows how to disappear, fight back, and dig up answers people would kill to keep buried. Cass is brilliant. Kendra is dangerous. Together, they're impossible to stop.

As they crisscross territories from the Northern Imperium to the California Confederacy, Cass and Kendra uncover pieces of a plan bigger than either of them—a plot that threatens to tip an already fragile world into chaos. To stop it, they'll have to rely on old contacts, new friends, and the kind of bond that's forged under fire and tested by every choice.

This isn't just about survival. It's about justice. It's about truth. And it's about proving that two people who refuse to back down can be enough to change everything.

Smart, fast-paced, and full of heart, *Cassidy Chronicles The Spark Before the Fire* kicks off a genre-blending saga that mixes political intrigue, breakneck action, and found-family loyalty with sharp dialogue and characters who refuse to be anything less than extraordinary.

For fans of *Firefly*, *The Expanse*, and clever women with their fingers on the trigger and their hearts on the line.

Read more at www.adamgaffenauthor.com.

About the Author

If you want strong FMCs who don't wait to be rescued, wit, and stories that will keep you up until 2am, then you're in the right place!

What *doesn't* Adam Gaffen write?

Well, hold on. He might be on it now.

So far his Cassidyverse contains Science Fiction, Fantasy, Thriller, and Rom-Com, with Dark Romance on the horizon.

He's a member of the Science Fiction Writers of America, and the Heinlein Society. He and his wife are owned by a pack of dogs and cats.

Read more at www.adamgaffenauthor.com.